Richard's face hardened.

"But you told us you..."

"You may have t... ...y," Elizabeth countered. Her conscience prodded her. Of course they had. Wasn't that exactly what she'd intended?

She sat straighter in her chair and looked squarely at them. While she felt they had brought this on themselves, she knew they deserved an explanation.

"It's all because you were pressing so hard to attach me to someone out here. I thought perhaps I could put a stop to it if you thought I was unavailable. I only said that to—"

"You lied!" Richard slammed his fist on the table, rattling the untouched breakfast dishes.

"Lied!" Letitia echoed. She covered her face with her hands and sank into her chair, loud sobs racking her body. "What are we to do, Richard? Is it too late to talk to Timothy?"

"I don't understand." Elizabeth raised her voice to be heard over Letitia's wails. "I apologize for any misunderstanding, but I fail to see—"

"That's just it." Richard's harsh tone cut across her words. "You don't see at all."

CAROL COX is a native of Arizona whose time is devoted to being a pastor's wife, keeping up with her college-age son's schedule, home schooling her young daughter, and serving as a church pianist, youth worker, and 4-H leader. She loves any activity she can share with her family in addition to her own pursuits in reading, crafts and local history. She also has had several novels and novellas published. Carol and her family make their home in northern Arizona.

Books by Carol Cox

HEARTSONG PRESENTS
HP264—Journey Toward Home
HP344—The Measure of a Man
HP452—Season of Hope
HP479—Cross My Heart

Land of Promise

Carol Cox

Heartsong Presents

A note from the Author:

I love to hear from my readers! You may correspond with me by writing:

> **Carol Cox**
> **Author Relations**
> **PO Box 719**
> **Uhrichsville, OH 44683**

ISBN 1-58660-998-X

LAND OF PROMISE

Our mission is to publish and distribute inspirational products offering exceptional value and biblical encouragement to the masses.

All Scripture quotations are taken from the King James Version of the Bible.

All of the characters and events in this book are fictitious. Any resemblance to actual persons, living or dead, or to actual events is purely coincidental.

PRINTED IN THE U.S.A.

prologue

Richard Bartlett leaned into the biting wind as he walked along, hating the wind, hating the cold, and finding no beauty in the brilliant streaks of rose and gold that tinged the late afternoon sky. The letter tucked into his waistcoat pocket crackled with every step, reminding him of his dilemma. Should he tell his wife that fool of a girl had written again, proposing a visit? And if he did, how should he break it to her? Letitia was hard enough to please in the best of times, but with her laid up now, and after their recent trouble, she was more sharp-tongued than ever. With his head turned down, chin tucked into the woolen scarf around his neck, he paid little heed to the rugged beauty around him.

A stocky figure stepped out of the shadows, planting its solid bulk directly in the preoccupied man's path, not flinching when the inevitable collision came.

"Why don't you watch where you're. . ." Richard broke off, realizing who he had run into. His face flushed, then cooled. "Timothy! I'm sorry. I didn't see you." He tried a weak laugh that didn't quite come off.

The shorter man adjusted the bowler hat the impact had knocked askew and rolled his cigar from one corner of his mouth to the other. "No problem, my friend. No problem at all." He waved his hand in a magnanimous gesture. "You look like a man with a lot on his mind." Timothy's shrewd blue eyes had noted Richard's involuntary start, and the ends of his handlebar mustache twitched upward in a satisfied smile. He hooked his thumbs in the pockets of his waistcoat in a comfortable, habitual gesture. "And probably with good reason." His eyes narrowed appraisingly. "Things haven't been going well for you lately, have they, Richard?"

Richard eyed Timothy's florid face suspiciously. Did a hidden meaning lie beyond the sympathetic words? He drew his handkerchief from his coat pocket and patted his forehead, despising the way his hands shook. "You're speaking of my wife's accident, of course," he replied, willing his voice to remain steady. "It was a shock, naturally, but the doctor assures us she'll recover in time." He pressed his lips together in irritation. Did Timothy deliberately smoke those cigars to veil his face in the dense cloud of smoke? Richard wouldn't put it past him. Timothy seldom missed an opportunity to put others at a disadvantage.

"Ah, Richard, Richard." Timothy's sorrowful tone grated on Richard's nerves. "I can understand a man having to maintain his pride, even in a situation like this. But you should know you can confide in me." He patted Richard's shoulder solicitously. "Walk with me," he said, nodding across the street to the broad plaza. "It will do you good to unburden yourself."

"Really, Timothy, I must get home. My wife will worry."

The blue eyes took on a glint of steely gray. "Then let us say that it would be to your advantage to talk to me, Richard. . . and to your disadvantage not to." The voice sounded no less menacing for its gentle tone. "Come walk with me." For all Richard's advantage in height, it was his shorter companion who radiated confidence and power as they strolled across the open area.

Richard felt his stomach tighten, as though preparing to ward off a blow. How much did Timothy know? How much more could he guess?

"A lovely place, this." Timothy nodded approvingly at the square set aside by the territorial capital's founders to provide a community gathering place. "A natural spot for two friends to cross going home in the evening, but with no place for listening ears to hide." He slowed and turned to face Richard. "How long do you think it will be before people find out you're destitute?"

The directness of the question took Richard's breath away. "I don't know what you—"

"Come, come." Timothy's voice registered impatience now. "If you think you can bluster your way through with everyone else, you can try that and see how far it gets you. But you're talking to me now, Richard, and I *know.*" He breathed the last word in an ominous whisper. "You invested everything you had in that mining stock Josh Wheeler was selling. Everything," he emphasized. "And the stock and the mine both turned out to be a sham. And instead of making a fortune, you're left penniless." He smiled at the shock on Richard's face and breathed out another wreath of cigar smoke.

"Not a pretty picture, is it? You're a political appointee out here, the same as me. The government has entrusted the running of this territory to the likes of us. How do you think they'll feel about your ability to manage a role in territorial government when you can't manage your own money?"

"I'm not the only one Wheeler took in." Richard made an effort to rise to his own defense. "There were plenty of others."

Timothy nodded slowly, as though weighing the statement. "True. But none of the others invested everything he had in the world. And none of the others had already lost one fortune before ever coming west." He chuckled at Richard's gaping mouth. "Did you think no one would ever learn of that?" he asked gently, then shook his head. "Knowledge is power, Richard. Remember that. I've made it my business to be a very knowledgeable man."

"Just what do you intend to do with that knowledge?" Richard's voice came out in a hoarse rasp, forced through a throat that had gone dry. Timothy's love of power was legendary, his use of it notorious. If word of Richard's folly spread through the frontier community, he would never be able to look people in the eye again, much less hold on to public office. And how many more fresh beginnings could a man in his fifties expect to have?

"That's entirely up to you," Timothy responded. "Personally, I would hate to see you humiliated and sent off in disgrace. We've worked well together in the past; I think we can do so in the future. Provided you're still here, of course," he added casually.

Richard fought to breathe, laboring against the tight band constricting his chest. "All right. What, exactly, do you want from me?"

"Ah, now we're getting down to business!" Timothy's face was wreathed in a genial smile, radiating goodwill. The sight turned Richard's stomach. "You've met my son, haven't you?" Timothy asked abruptly.

Richard nodded, wondering at the change of subject. "Several times. Why?"

"He's the pride of my life," Timothy answered, "a fitting heir for the legacy I'm building for him. Even if he doesn't care about it yet." He tossed the cigar stub down and ground it out with a vicious dig of his heel. "He's a stubborn lad. At the moment, he tells me he doesn't have an interest in politics, but that will change. And when it does, all the groundwork I've laid will be waiting for him. He'll be able to step right into a life of power, wealth, and influence." His voice trailed off, and he stood staring at the darkening sky as if watching his words become reality.

Richard shifted uncomfortably. "But what does that have to do with—"

"Up to now," Timothy continued as if Richard hadn't spoken, "he's shown no interest in marriage, but mark my word, it's only a matter of time until some woman realizes what a catch he is and sets her sights on him. When that happens,

I don't want to see him as the target of one of these back-woods bumpkins. I won't have it!" Timothy's eyes glittered menacingly. "He needs a wife who will be an asset to him, who knows how to move in the right social circles, not one of the pathetic rubes you'll find around here."

"I still don't see—"

"I need a girl," Timothy stated. "And you're going to provide one for me." He threw back his head and bellowed with laughter at Richard's look of utter astonishment, his ample stomach shaking beneath the gaudy vest. "Think it through," he commanded. "You have connections back in Philadelphia, and at the moment, you still have a reputation worth upholding. Surely you know some girl of good family who would be a match for my boy. One of refinement, whose background would enhance his political career."

He watched the unbidden play of emotions on Richard's face and smiled serenely. "I thought so. Then here is the bargain: Get her out here to Arizona Territory. You could use your wife's injuries as an excuse. Arrange for her to meet my son. Tell her what a bright future he has."

Timothy's voice dropped to a murmur so low that Richard had to strain to hear him. "Help them get acquainted. Give them every opportunity to spend time together. She'll be such a contrast to the backward females he sees here, he'll be captivated by her. And if you do your job well, I expect her to be equally fascinated by the prospect of marriage to him.

"Make that marriage a reality, Richard, and not only will I hold my tongue about your disastrous financial blunder, but I will reward you handsomely." He leaned forward and named a sum large enough to make Richard's eyes bulge.

Timothy eyed his companion closely, then nodded. "That is our arrangement. I get what I want; you get what you want, and no one is the wiser. Are we agreed?"

Richard's mind reeled. To go from the threat of exposure to the promise of restored wealth! To be able to offer Letitia the means of recouping their loss and getting back on their feet without losing face! She would grasp the opportunity as eagerly as he.

"Agreed," he said and shook Timothy's hand in a firm grip. He turned away and started for home once more, wiping his palm on his pant leg as soon as he was sure Timothy's back was turned. Once again, he patted his vest pocket, feeling the reassuring crackle of the letter, and smiled for the first time in weeks.

one

Elizabeth Simmons closed her bedroom door behind her and moved to the head of the curving staircase, casting a scornful glance at the glittering scene below. Brilliant ball gowns glowed like jewels on a black cloth against the men's dark evening dress, and the murmur of refined voices rose to Elizabeth's ears. The cream of Philadelphia society was present tonight, a coup that would further enhance her mother's already high social standing.

Mama must be delighted, she thought sourly. Elizabeth surveyed the spectacle from her vantage point, wanting to delay her descent as long as possible. *Empty words, empty minds, empty people. What a waste of an evening!*

A slender figure in emerald velvet hurried to the foot of the stairs. "Elizabeth, come quickly!" Her sister Carrie's urgent voice floated upward. Light from the chandeliers caught the reddish glints in the young girl's hair, turning them to threads of burnished copper. "Mama's been asking and asking where you are, and she's beginning to get very cross."

Elizabeth watched her sister swirl back into the eddy of activity and gave a sigh of resignation. Like it or not, her presence was demanded. She moved down the staircase, the rustle of her sapphire satin gown barely audible over the swell of voices and the strains of music drifting from the ballroom.

Elizabeth braced herself for the ordeal of taking part in the mindless chatter that was a standard feature of her mother's social affairs. Seeing one of her mother's closest friends hovering at the foot of the stairs, she forced a smile. "Good evening, Mrs. Stephens. How nice to see you here."

"How nice of *you* to make time to come down and join us," the older woman returned with a glacial stare. "Really, Elizabeth, it's too bad of you. You know how much tonight means to your mother. After all the preparations the poor woman has made to ensure the success of this evening, you might at least make an effort not to embarrass her by your tardiness. Come along," she ordered, gripping Elizabeth's elbow with a proprietary air and propelling her forward. "You must let her know at once that you've decided to grace the festivities. The poor woman is quite distraught."

"Oh, you've found her." Both women turned at the sound of the rich baritone voice, and Elizabeth brightened at the sight of her neighbor, James Reilly.

"I've come to make sure Elizabeth is mingling with the guests. Would you be kind enough to let Mrs. Simmons know she has come down while I escort her to her duties?" James bent over Mrs. Stephens's blue-veined hand in a courtly gesture. "And may I say just how stunning you look tonight?"

Elizabeth's lips twitched in amusement at the sight of her unwelcome chaperone simpering with delight at James's attention. The older woman sailed off to carry the message to her friend, and James steered Elizabeth through the crowd.

"However did you manage to appear on the scene at just the right moment?" she asked, weaving her way through the sea of frock coats and voluminous skirts. "I wouldn't have been able to hold my tongue one second longer."

James threw back his head and laughed, drawing an admiring glance from more than one of the young ladies they passed. "You've never held your tongue about any issue you felt strongly about in all your life." He tucked her hand more firmly into the crook of his arm and gave it a squeeze. "It's one of the things I value most about you."

"I suppose you expect me to be grateful for that insufferably condescending remark?" Elizabeth sniffed, attempting a show of indignation belied by the curve of her lips. "Never mind. You do deserve some gratitude for rescuing me."

"Rescuing Muriel Stephens, you mean," James countered with a chuckle. "She'll never know what a narrow escape she had. Besides, if you'll recall, you once promised to marry me. That gives me a vested interest in your welfare."

Elizabeth snorted. "If *you'll* recall, that promise was made when I was all of four years old, and you were six. You're hardly likely to hold me to it now. Besides, you know very well I'm much too strong-minded for you." She turned left, toward the ballroom, then frowned when James guided her in the opposite direction. "Where are we going?"

"I promised you'd be mingling dutifully with the guests. But I didn't say which guests, did I?" James smiled, opening the library door and ushering Elizabeth inside.

"Here she is," he announced. A fire crackled in the hearth, silhouetting the two men who rose to bow in greeting. "Elizabeth, may I introduce Thomas Brady and Elliot Carpenter? Gentlemen, this is Miss Simmons."

"So this is the woman who has more on her mind than her next visit to the dressmaker?" Thomas Brady took the hand Elizabeth offered and quirked an eyebrow in James's direction. "You neglected to tell us she is also a delight to the eye, James."

Elizabeth snatched her hand away. "Don't praise my mind in one sentence, then insult my intelligence in the next, Mr. Brady. I'm quite aware of my physical shortcomings. My eyes and hair are a dreary brown, and I'm far too short of stature to be considered attractive, let alone beautiful. Fortunately, my value as a woman and as a child of God rests in my character and not my physical attributes."

Thomas Brady stood speechless, and James hooted with laughter at his friend's discomfiture. "I did mention that she was outspoken, didn't I?"

"And as always, you are a man of your word," Thomas

agreed, finding his voice again. "Miss Simmons, please accept my apology for what must have seemed gratuitous flattery. I would take issue with your assessment of yourself if I didn't fear offending you again, but I must say I am thoroughly intrigued, and I look forward to hearing the views of a woman of your perspicacity. And that," he said, raising his hand solemnly, "is the truth, the whole truth, and nothing but the truth."

Elizabeth searched his face, wondering if she were being made the butt of a masculine joke, but found no sign of duplicity. She smiled and extended her hand to his companion. "And you, Mr. Carpenter? Are you willing to exchange views with a mere woman?"

"I believe we shall meet on equal footing," he responded with a laugh. "Or if we do not meet as equals, it will be because your intelligence surpasses ours. I can see that I shall need to have all my wits about me so I am not totally outclassed."

"Shall we all sit down?" James asked as easily as if he were the master of the house. "Thomas, Elliot, and I have been discussing the issue of women's suffrage. I thought you could give us an articulate woman's view of the subject."

Elizabeth's pulse quickened. Maybe this evening wouldn't be a bore, after all. With a sense of anticipation, she settled herself in her father's favorite leather chair, prepared to hold forth on a cherished topic. The men drew up chairs in a semicircle facing hers, the two visitors placing theirs at a cautious distance. Elizabeth clasped her hands in her lap, back erect, and looked at her audience like a professor inspecting a new class of pupils.

"Giving women their due is hardly a new idea," she began. "Nearly thirty years ago, two American women went to the World Anti-slavery Convention in London. They were bona fide delegates, but because they were women, they were not allowed to participate. Imagine traveling all that way for such a worthy cause, only to be told you had to sit in a curtained-off area away from those taking an active part, merely because the people in charge didn't approve of your gender!"

She scrutinized each face, seeking their reactions. James nodded encouragingly, having heard this discourse before. Elliot Carpenter sat with his chair turned slightly away from her, propping his chin on one hand. His expression was carefully neutral, but Elizabeth thought she detected an amused glint in his eyes. Thomas Brady leaned forward, elbows on his knees, apparently weighing her words carefully. She focused her attention on him.

"I'm sure you've heard their names before, gentlemen. Lucretia Mott and Elizabeth Cady Stanton will long be remembered for the part they held." Elizabeth tried to stem her excitement at the thought of her heroines. "Eight long years passed before they convened the first women's rights convention in Seneca Falls. Even then, their success was measured more in the sense of accomplishment for taking this momentous step than in realizing any tangible gains.

"Explain to me, if you can, why so many northern men could recognize the iniquity of slavery but continue to hold their sisters, wives, and daughters in what is tantamount to a benevolent captivity?"

"Oh, I say! Don't you think that's a bit harsh?" Thomas expostulated. "Look at the ladies here tonight. I don't believe one of them would think of themselves as deprived. When do you think was the last time any of them were denied anything?"

"Exactly my point, Mr. Brady. They've been spoiled and cosseted, treated more like pampered pets than thinking human beings. That in itself denies them the ability to think for themselves. And women *are* thinking creatures." Out of the corner of her eye, she noted Elliot Carpenter straightening in his chair and suppressed a satisfied smile. He was listening now, really listening. And she had barely gotten started.

"Women have proven their worth over and over again. Elizabeth Blackwell won her medical degree in 1849. Was that a feat some 'frivolous woman' could have accomplished? And only a few years ago during the war, Elizabeth Cady Stanton helped organize the Women's Loyal National League. Those women managed to gather over three hundred thousand signatures on a petition demanding that the Senate abolish slavery by a constitutional amendment. Three hundred thousand! That was not the work of a group of tea-sipping females who had nothing but cotton wool between their ears.

"God gave us minds, gentlemen. I believe He did not equip us with intelligence and plenty of drive if He did not intend for us to use them."

"But you've just proven women do use their minds and in very profitable ways." Elliot Carpenter scooted his chair closer to Elizabeth's and faced her squarely. "Having the right to mark a ballot won't change any of these God-given attributes."

Elizabeth's temper flared at the sight of his self-satisfied smile. Making a deliberate effort to keep her indignation in check, she held his gaze with hers, measuring her words with care. "Less than a century ago, our forefathers were able to use their gifts and abilities, but they felt strongly about being allowed to govern themselves. I see no difference, Mr. Carpenter."

"I see a great difference!" Elliot sputtered, shaken from his easy calm. "That was about taxation and commerce and—"

"And self-respect," Elizabeth put in. "As thinking men, they wanted the opportunity to have a say in matters that concerned them. Thinking women want no less."

The debate continued in earnest, with Thomas and Elliot voicing their long-held beliefs as though talking to another man and Elizabeth fielding their questions and objections with ease.

The library door swung open abruptly. "I thought I heard voices," said a shrill female voice. "Who is in here?"

The four occupants of the room jumped as if caught in some misdeed. Elizabeth blinked, realizing for the first time how low the fire burned in the hearth. "It's just James and me, Mother," she called. "And two of his friends. We've been talking."

Cora Simmons stepped through the doorway, lips parted

in disbelief. "Do you mean to tell me that this is where you've been all night? I was given to understand that you were fulfilling your responsibilities in attending to my guests. Have you been shut up in here the whole time? With three men?" Her piercing voice rose to a higher pitch with every syllable.

James and his visitors took their cue, rising with alacrity to bid their hostess good night. While James and Elliot Carpenter were thus occupied, Thomas Brady took advantage of the opportunity to bow over Elizabeth's hand.

"Thank you for a most informative evening," he said. "You have given me much to think about. And since I'm about to leave," he added, one corner of his mouth twitching upward, "I will repeat my former statement. Despite your own opinion, Miss Simmons, you are a lovely lady. Perhaps when you look in the mirror, you have never noticed the way your hair glistens with a chestnut sheen or watched your eyes flash green fire when your emotions are aroused. But I have, and I am utterly captivated." He gave a quick nod and turned away before Elizabeth could think of a suitable retort.

Thomas joined his companions in thanking Mrs. Simmons for an enjoyable evening. Elizabeth heard her mother acknowledge their speeches politely but noted her decidedly cool response. In the dim glow from the fireplace, with the only other light filtering in from the hall, the light gray streaks were no longer visible in hair that had once been a vibrant red. Nor could anyone see the lines of discontent etched on her face. Cora's slender build looked almost girlish, and in the waning light, Elizabeth could glimpse traces of her mother's former beauty.

"I'll see you gentlemen to the door," Cora said. "The other guests have already taken their leave." She herded the three subdued men through the open doorway, then turned to face her daughter. "Elizabeth, you will remain here until I return. . .with your father. This unseemly behavior of yours has gone too far."

Elizabeth watched the door close, knowing a storm was about to break. How many times had they played out a similar scene in the past? This time, though, the play would have an entirely different ending. She moved to the fireplace and checked behind the mantel clock, reassuring herself the papers were where she had left them that afternoon. Her original intention had been to show them to her family tomorrow, but it appeared her plan would have to be revised.

Even so, she would make sure tonight's confrontation would be as much to her advantage as possible. Elizabeth stirred the fire back to life with the poker and lit two lamps, placing them on low tables and arranging the seating to best suit her strategy. By the time she heard voices in the hallway outside, she stood ready, determined to take control of the confrontation to come.

Her mother entered the room first, eyes blazing. Elizabeth's father followed, an obviously unwilling participant. Before the door closed, Carrie slipped into the room with her usual quick grace, with Virginia, the middle sister, gliding in behind her. Carrie moved at once to a pocket of shadow near the bookcase, while Virginia positioned herself near their mother, her smirk indicating she planned to enjoy the fun.

Elizabeth acted quickly before she could lose her advantage. "Sit here, please, Mother," she said, pointing to the comfortable leather chair she had recently vacated. Cora gaped at the order but sank into the seat indicated. "Carrie, Virginia, you may sit in the wing chairs." Elizabeth smiled inwardly, watching her sisters' predictable placement, with Virginia taking the chair nearest their mother and Carrie scooting slightly closer to Elizabeth.

"Father—"

"I'll stand, thank you." His tone sounded gruff, but he smiled at his eldest daughter with genuine affection, tilting up the corners of his mustache and puffing his rounded cheeks. The smile faded when he turned to face his wife. "What's this all about, Cora? Can't it wait until morning?"

"No, Monroe, it cannot." Cora had recovered from her initial confusion. "We need to discuss the disgraceful behavior of your daughter."

"Which one?" The feigned ignorance in those hazel eyes so like her own made Elizabeth want to burst out laughing. As if he didn't know! Creamy-skinned Virginia, whose only interests in life consisted of social prominence and an ample supply of creature comforts, was very much the product of her mother's upbringing. Cora would never find fault with her. And Carrie, with her gentle spirit, might agree with most of Elizabeth's views but would never openly defy her mother. Tonight's culprit would be the same daughter who had always caused her mother distress, and well Monroe knew that.

Apparently, Cora thought so, too. Her nostrils flared as she drew a deep breath and pressed her lips together. Elizabeth, realizing she might soon lose her opportunity, hurried to seize the moment.

"I'm glad you're all here," she began, ignoring her mother's gasp of surprise and the appreciative twinkle in her father's eyes. "I had planned to discuss something with you tomorrow morning, but I believe this would be a better time." She stepped across to the fireplace and drew two envelopes from behind the mantel clock. "Both of these letters arrived in this afternoon's post. I've only opened the one addressed to me, but I believe I can tell you what you'll find in the other one."

"Whatever are you babbling about?" Cora stretched out her hand in a silent demand for the letters, but Elizabeth moved away from her. "*You* are the topic of discussion here, young lady, and those letters can be of no possible interest to us right now."

Monroe rocked back on his heels, eyeing Elizabeth shrewdly. "She's a sharp girl, Cora. Let her have her say." He nodded at Elizabeth. "All right, tell us what's in the letter."

"As I said, I haven't opened this one," she said, handing the envelope to him. "It's addressed to you and Mother, from Mr. and Mrs. Bartlett. I believe when you read it, you'll find an account of how Mrs. Bartlett suffered severe injuries in a fall."

"Letitia?" For once, her mother seemed concerned about someone other than herself. "What happened? Will she recover?"

"According to Mr. Bartlett's letter, she slipped on a patch of ice on the path outside their home and fractured her right arm when she tried to break her fall. She landed up against the porch steps, and the force of the blow cracked a rib and caused some deep bruising." Elizabeth watched her mother's face grow pale and took pity on her. "They are sure she will recover, but it will take time."

"Poor Letitia!" Cora pressed her hand to her heaving bosom. "However will she manage out in that forsaken wilderness? Why Richard insisted on dragging her out to such a horrid wasteland, I will never know."

"He didn't have much choice," Monroe answered drily. "Running a cotton mill during the war was not a money-making proposition. That political appointment came at an opportune time."

"But to take a refined woman like that to a place inhabited only by ruffians and savages!" Cora dabbed at her eyes with a lace handkerchief. "I've said it before and I'll say it again—it was a heartless thing to do."

"And how does this concern you, Elizabeth?" Monroe asked. "You said this had some bearing on your wanting to talk to us."

"It does." Elizabeth drew a deep breath, studying the faces of her family. "You're quite right, Mother. While Mrs. Bartlett is expected to recover, she requires a great deal of help. This letter," she said, holding up the remaining missive, "is a request for me to travel to Arizona Territory to give her the help she needs."

two

Cora's shriek of dismay was the only sound in the room. Carrie and Virginia stared at Elizabeth wordlessly, and even Monroe seemed taken aback. "Why you?" he asked incredulously. "Granted, we've known the Bartletts for years, but you've never been particularly close to them. I wouldn't have guessed they were especially fond of you."

"Actually, this was more my doing than theirs." Elizabeth squared her shoulders, framing her answer carefully. She was painfully aware that a misstep now might prove to be her undoing. "Last December, I wrote to the Bartletts, asking if I might visit them for a time." Cora uttered a strangled cry. Elizabeth flinched but went on. "I received no response, and I didn't know whether my message had reached them or not. I wrote again a month ago, repeating my request. My letter arrived shortly after Mrs. Bartlett was injured. This time, Mr. Bartlett was quick to reply."

"You asked to go there?" Bewilderment flooded Carrie's features. "But why, Elizabeth?"

Blessing her sister for providing the very opening she needed, Elizabeth gathered her courage and plunged ahead. "I want to see what Arizona has to offer. The territory was created only four years ago. It's young, wide open, and waiting for people of initiative and drive. It's a perfect place to test a person's mettle and see if their dreams—if *my* dreams—can succeed."

Virginia brushed her auburn curls back in a languorous gesture. "And once you've thoroughly explored the possibilities, I suppose you'll come back and enlighten those of us without your spirit of adventure," she taunted.

"That's just it," Elizabeth stated. "I'm not coming back."

This time even Monroe gasped. "My plans have been made for some time," she continued before anyone else could speak. "I only needed the opportunity to set them in motion. I'll be able to get acquainted with the area while I'm tending to Mrs. Bartlett. That will give me the chance I need to see what goods or services the territory needs. When I'm ready, I'll set up my own business and see what I can make of myself."

"And just how do you plan to support yourself?" Cora drew herself erect. "Do you think for one minute your father and I will finance this mad expedition?"

"I don't need your backing, Mother," Elizabeth said quietly. "Don't forget the money Grandmother Simmons left me. It's mine, free and clear, to do with as I wish. And since I'm a year past my twenty-first birthday, I don't have to ask anyone's permission to do this."

For a full minute, only the ticking of the mantel clock intruded on the stunned silence. Then Carrie spoke, her blue-green eyes wide with dismay. "Oh, Elizabeth, I can't imagine it! You, all alone out there in a savage country. However will you manage?" Her voice softened to a dreamy sigh. "But what a glorious adventure it will be!"

Elizabeth smiled her appreciation at Carrie and glanced toward her other sister. Virginia contented herself with lounging back in her chair and expressing her feelings with a disdainful smirk.

Monroe's face wore a faraway look. "It reminds me of the way I felt when I was young," he murmured. "Opportunities abounded for a person with grit and determination—those were exciting days."

"Have you all gone quite mad?" Cora screeched, digging her fingers into the damask upholstery. She turned to Monroe, directing the brunt of her fury at him. "You're to blame for this! You've treated her more like a son than a daughter since the day she was born. What kind of father lets his daughter accompany him to his factory from the time she could walk? I ask you, what possible interest could a decent young lady have in metalworks? Monroe, I have done my best and been thwarted at every turn. I have made every effort to bring Elizabeth up in a genteel fashion, yet you've continued to discuss business matters and current affairs with her as though she were one of your cronies.

"As if that weren't enough, your mother filled her head with all sorts of unfeminine notions she gleaned from her friendship with that Stanton woman. I told you no good would come of it when she left that sum of money to Elizabeth. I hold you completely accountable for this!" she fumed, red-faced, her bosom heaving.

Monroe's forbidding expression could have been chiseled out of granite. "If you're saying I'm responsible for honing Elizabeth's mind and developing her character, Cora, I'll take that as a compliment. She has a fine intellect and a keen wit, not to mention a good head for business. More than once, I've profited from her insight. And as far as my mother's influence is concerned, I can only say I'm sorry she didn't have a greater impact on all our daughters."

Ignoring Cora's gasp of outrage, he stared into the fire for a moment, then turned to Elizabeth, his features softening. "I'll miss you, my dear, but I wish you every success. You have my blessing."

With a rush of gratitude, Elizabeth flung herself into his open arms.

❧

Three days later, Elizabeth stood before her open trunk, trying to wedge in one more dress. Carrie added her weight to the trunk lid and together they managed to close the latch.

"How I envy you, Elizabeth." Carrie settled herself on the edge of the bed with a little flounce, her aquamarine eyes alight with excitement. "If only I had the courage, I'd go with you."

Elizabeth whirled from the dressing table where she was placing the last of her personal effects into a reticule. "Would you, Carrie? I have plenty of money to pay your way. If the Bartletts don't have room for both of us, I'll find a place for you to live until we get our bearings."

Carrie shook her head ruefully. The red-gold tendrils framing her fine-boned face caught the shaft of morning sunlight streaming through the window. "I know myself too well. Though I admire you with all my heart, I don't have your strength of character. Much as I hate to admit it, I'm far too much a product of Mama's upbringing. I'd never have the gumption to give up the comforts of home and go off like that, with only myself to rely upon."

The young girl sighed and wrapped her arms around her knees. "I shall have to experience all my adventures through you, so you must be sure to write often and tell me absolutely everything that is going on. Promise?"

"I promise." Elizabeth bent to give her sister a warm hug.

"What a touching scene," Virginia said from the doorway, her lip curled in a contemptuous sneer. "But after that exhibition of yours the other night, I should have expected nothing less than high drama." She moved to a pile of dresses next to Elizabeth's trunk and fingered the rich fabrics. "You're leaving these behind? I'd try to feel sorry for you, but out where you're going you'll be more in need of homespun and buckskin, won't you?"

"Contrary to what you and Mother believe," Elizabeth retorted, "what lies within a person's heart is far more important than what clothes the surface. My wardrobe is perfectly adequate."

Virginia shrugged and moved to a vantage point from which she could look out the large window. "I believe I'll have my things moved into your room once you've gone. I always did envy your view, and this room is much larger than mine." She pivoted, tapping her finger against her lips while she considered the possibilities. "Yes, it will do nicely, even if I won't be here much longer myself."

Carrie's mouth dropped open, and Elizabeth felt her own curiosity rising. Curiosity and irritation, mixed. Virginia never could resist tantalizing others when she had news. "And just where are you going?" Elizabeth asked. "I haven't heard you mention any plans."

"You're not the only one who can have aspirations and keep secrets, dear sister." Virginia's expression reminded Elizabeth of a sleek, haughty cat. "Before the year is out, I have every intention of being the mistress of my own home."

Carrie gasped and bounced to her feet. "Are you engaged, Virginia? Who is it?"

Virginia leaned against the bedpost. "I don't know yet, but I expect to soon." She laughed at Carrie's consternation. "Sister dear, there are at least three highly eligible gentlemen vying for my hand at the moment. All I need to do is make up my mind which one has the most to offer me."

"You mean which one you truly love, don't you?" Carrie asked, a doubtful note in her voice.

Virginia tossed back her mane of russet hair and laughed. "You are such a child! Surely I knew more about life when I was sixteen. Love has little to do with it. All three of them adore me."

"And that's all that matters to you, isn't it?" Elizabeth planted her fists on her hips and glared at her sister. "Virginia, have you ever spent a moment considering anyone's happiness but your own? Do you honestly think these three suitors of yours have nothing better to do than dance attendance on you for the rest of their days?"

Virginia preened herself in front of Elizabeth's looking glass. "I have two very simple criteria for choosing a husband. One, I must be the most important thing in his life. Two, he must be able to maintain me in a lifestyle comparable or superior to what Papa has provided."

Elizabeth shook her head and snorted in disgust. "It's obvious you've placed your own importance before that of everyone else—including God. You'll never find happiness until He has first place in your life. You've heard Pastor Whitcomb say so often enough."

"And what about you?" Virginia flung back, for once shaken from her air of unruffled superiority. "You're going off to see 'what you can make of yourself.' How does that focus on anyone but you?"

Elizabeth stiffened. "It's not the same," she countered. "It's not the same at all."

❧

The stagecoach swayed along the uneven road, bouncing over a rut with a jolt that snapped Elizabeth's drooping head against the frame. The impact jarred her awake, and she brushed a hand across her eyes before looking out the window to take note of her surroundings.

It had been nearly two weeks since she'd left Philadelphia. Two weary, bone-rattling weeks. Elizabeth stretched as much as she could in the confined space, careful to avoid contact with the army captain who got on at Fort Wingate and the two hopeful miners bound for the gold fields. The train ride to Kansas City hadn't been too bad, although she'd grown heartily tired of her various garrulous seatmates long before it ended. The stage, though, had been a different story. Surely the contraption had been designed for the express purpose of shaking the passengers loose at every joint.

Elizabeth had occupied herself by watching the changing landscape, marveling as the gently rolling hills gave way to the vast plains, then to the majestically rugged western mountain country. The red cliffs near Santa Fe had delighted her, and she reveled in the many hues playing across the hills. Even the accounts she pored over in the eastern newspapers had not prepared her for the vivid purples, golds, and crimsons. The land opened wide before her, wild and untamed, with stunning vistas on every side, and her breath quickened in anticipation. Here was her land of promise. Would she be equal to its challenge?

She closed her eyes, reliving the scene before she boarded the train, with James and her father fussing over her like mother hens, anxious to see her baggage stowed away properly and that she had everything she needed for the journey. Elizabeth stifled a wry laugh, remembering how her mother had come down with an attack of the vapors shortly before her departure, conveniently assuring that Carrie and Virginia would have to stay home to care for her.

No matter. Elizabeth and Carrie had said their good-byes the night before. Not having to deal with Cora's cold disapproval and Virginia's scorn made the parting just that much easier.

She had been pleasantly surprised when Pastor Whitcomb came to bid her farewell. He'd pushed his way through the crowd at the last minute, the displaced strands of silver-gray hair marring his usually immaculate appearance. "My dear," he puffed, mopping his brow with a handkerchief, "I feared I had already missed you."

Elizabeth smiled at the man who had been her spiritual teacher since she was a toddler. "It was good of you to come."

"How could I miss the opportunity to say good-bye to one of my favorite parishioners?" His eyes held an affectionate gleam. "You have always shown courage and determination, Elizabeth. Independence, too. All very admirable qualities when exercised properly." His genial face then took on a more somber expression. "Just be certain you do not try to become independent of God."

"We're gettin' close, aren't we?" The cracked voice of one of the miners broke into her thoughts, and she opened her eyes again. They had entered the broad valley now. The crisp breeze swept through the open coach windows. Elizabeth declined the captain's offer to lower the window canvas. Even though patches of snow lay under the tall pines, the bright sun's warmth was invigorating.

"About two hours more, I figure," the miner's companion answered. "I'll be right glad to get down out of this vee-hicle and start finding those nuggets."

Elizabeth shifted position slightly, trying to ease her knotted muscles. Soon this interminable trip would be over and the real adventure would begin.

It was closer to three hours later by Elizabeth's estimation when the stage finally, blessedly pulled to a stop in Prescott. The captain immediately pushed the door open and sprang to the ground, then turned to hand Elizabeth down.

She tottered out on unsteady limbs and stepped away from the coach, surveying her new home. Clapboard storefronts lined the street before her, and across it was a broad, open square. The cross street to her right seemed to be a hub of activity, judging from the steady stream of men entering and leaving its buildings. Through their swinging doors came raucous laughter and the tinny sounds of pianos played by inexpert hands. A flicker of uncertainty assailed her. Where could Mr. Bartlett be?

"Just arrived, have you, Dearie?"

Elizabeth turned to face the diminutive figure at her elbow. The woman's wrinkled face broadened in a kind smile. "Of course you have," she chuckled, "seeing as how I saw you step down off the stage. Isn't anyone here to meet you?"

"I was expecting someone, yes," Elizabeth admitted. Seeing the woman tilt her head in curiosity, she added, "I've come to help care for an acquaintance who's ill."

"Bless you, now! She must be grateful to have a faithful friend like you." Her eyes darkened, and her gaze fastened on a point beyond Elizabeth's shoulder. "And what is he up to, I wonder?" she muttered. "Supposed to be tending to government business, but more likely coming straight from a faro game, by the looks of him."

Elizabeth pivoted and followed her companion's gaze. Richard Bartlett hurried toward her from the direction of the saloons.

"Elizabeth!" he called. "You've arrived at last. Welcome to Arizona Territory." He cast a nervous look at the woman next to her. "Good afternoon, Mrs. Ehle."

The tiny woman narrowed her eyes and grasped Elizabeth's elbow. "Is it her you've come to take care of? His wife?"

Elizabeth nodded mutely.

Mrs. Ehle shook her head. "You seem like far too nice a girl to be abused by that old Tartar." She patted Elizabeth's arm. "I'll be praying for you, Dearie. You'll need it!"

three

With a shake of her head, the old woman walked on down the street. Elizabeth stared in bewilderment, then turned to face Richard Bartlett. A sour expression crossed his face, which was replaced by an ingratiating smile when he saw her looking at him.

"You'll find the people here more coarse than what you're used to," he said with a short laugh. "Which are your bags?" She pointed out her carpetbag, and he hefted it with a grunt. "I'll arrange for your trunk to be sent to the house. Let's get you settled in."

Elizabeth blinked, then broke into a smile. At home, she would have been met by a carriage and driven to their destination in fine style. She had never expected to walk to her new dwelling. But this was the West, her new home. She would learn to adapt to the way things were done here.

She studied her companion covertly while they walked along. More gray sprinkled his hair than when she last saw him. His face seemed thinner, more pinched, the beaklike nose even more prominent. Perhaps she should attribute it to the natural effects of aging.

Richard led her one block east, then turned north. "This seems odd to you, I know. So different from what you are accustomed to. But give it a chance, my dear. You'll come to appreciate the place and, someday, its people."

He leaned toward her, and she caught the sour smell of liquor on his breath, faint but unmistakable. Her nose wrinkled at the pungent odor, and she experienced a vague sense of unease. It couldn't be later than three in the afternoon. Had Richard drunk spirits in the middle of the day back in

Philadelphia? She didn't think so, but as her father had pointed out, she had never been close to the Bartletts.

"I can't tell you how happy we are to have you here." Richard's lips parted in a grimace she supposed was meant to look like a welcoming smile. His geniality seemed at variance with what Elizabeth remembered of him. She tucked that impression away for future reference and forced a polite smile in return. She would only be with the Bartletts temporarily. She didn't have to understand them, just appreciate this means of getting to know Prescott.

Still, his jaunty tone struck a sour note. Perhaps it was due to relief at having the responsibility for his wife's care lifted from his shoulders. But Richard's tone sounded like a man ready to celebrate.

❧

Michael O'Roarke crossed the plaza with quick steps, making no attempt to shield his face from the brisk April wind. He could have sent his clerk to run the errand for him, but spending hours bent over his desk checking freight manifests had made him long for a taste of the outdoors. Verifying Clifford Johnson's latest order might be a menial task, but the trek across town gave him the chance to stretch his legs and fill his lungs with the bracing air.

Hands in his pockets, he crossed the plaza. Strains of music wafted from one of the saloons that lined the opposite side of Montezuma Street, otherwise known as Whiskey Row.

"Each time I see the sun set
Beyond the distant hills. . ."

The clear soprano voice rang out against the tinny piano notes.

Without conscious volition, Michael's steps slowed, and he stopped to listen. The sadness in the singer's voice fit the haunting lyrics to a T. And well it should. Michael could imagine no more sordid existence for a young woman than to be caught up in the vice and degradation of saloon life.

The new Arizona Territory had been called a land of opportunity, and the name held true for many. For others, though, like this plaintive-voiced singer, it could only be a miserable end.

The song ended, but to Michael, the last few longing notes seemed to hang in the clear spring air. How could anyone connected with the saloons and what went on there possess so pure a voice? Maybe a better question would be: How could anyone so gifted sink to such depths?

Only God had the answers. Michael breathed a quick prayer for the unknown singer. He couldn't solve such philosophical questions this afternoon. He could, however, take care of his own responsibilities.

He waved to the driver of the departing stagecoach and crossed Gurley Street in its wake, wondering if the stage had brought yet more fortune seekers to the capital. Adventure and the quest for personal advancement seemed to draw politically ambitious men out of the woodwork. Michael ought to know; his father had been one of the first.

At the next corner, he stopped to get his bearings. He had only been to Johnson's place once before. Was it farther along this street, or did he need to go east one block farther?

Michael rubbed warmth back into his fingers and wished he hadn't left his gloves back in his desk drawer. Turning east, he took a few more steps, then noticed a man and woman walking toward him. He headed their way, planning to ask for directions.

On second glance, he recognized the man and took a quick turn down a side street instead. Richard Bartlett. In Michael's opinion, the man embodied all the worst qualities of those who came to Arizona seeking their fortunes. He'd rather spend extra time finding Cliff Johnson than exchange words with someone for whom he had so little respect.

❧

Richard stopped in midstride and waved his free hand. Elizabeth followed his gaze but saw only a dark-haired man striding away from them. She cast a quizzical glance at Richard, who shrugged.

"I thought to introduce you to one of our local young men. He must not have seen us. Another time, perhaps. As I was saying, we're glad to have you here. In time, I'm sure you will come to appreciate Prescott's finer qualities." He grinned at her again.

Once more, Richard's buoyant tone seemed out of place and reminded Elizabeth of a patent remedy salesman she'd heard years before. Could she attribute his odd demeanor to his drinking and his drinking to worry about his wife's health? If so, that should settle down now that she was here to help. And what if it didn't?

No, she wouldn't borrow trouble. Right now she felt exhausted from her trip, very glad to be at journey's end, and eager to rest up a bit before taking over her duties with Letitia. Time enough later on to deal with Richard's drinking problem, if he did indeed have one.

Her thoughts were interrupted when Richard stopped before a white house with dark blue shutters. "We're home," he announced.

Elizabeth took in the neat frame building. If her acquaintances back home expected her to take up residence in a log cabin or primitive adobe shack, they would be sadly disappointed. The Bartlett home could have been transplanted straight from some Midwestern street, from the neat bay window to the rose that twined along the porch railing.

Inside, the front door opened onto the parlor, where Elizabeth recognized a few pieces from the Bartletts' home in Philadelphia. A sudden wave of weariness swept over her.

"This will be your room. I hope it's satisfactory." Richard turned down a short hallway and set her carpetbag down just inside the door on the right.

Tired as she was, Elizabeth would have been happy with the barest of essentials. The sunlit room with its white eyelet curtains and matching bed covers provided a balm to her travel-weary soul. The soft bed called to her to nestle within its depths.

"Letitia's room is this way. She'll be anxious to see you."

Of course. This was, after all, the reason she had come. She shook her head to clear it and accompanied Richard to the room opposite hers. Her own needs would have to wait.

It took a moment for her eyes to adjust to the dimness and make out Letitia, who was propped up against a stack of pillows. In contrast to her own room, awash with light, the sickroom drapes were closed, giving the room a suffocating quality. Elizabeth approached the bed.

"Look who's here," Richard boomed in a jovial voice. "Elizabeth has arrived at last."

Letitia turned her head and lifted her hand from her cocoon of blankets. She grasped Elizabeth's arm with fingers that clutched like a bird's claw. "Bless you for coming, my dear."

Elizabeth eased free of the woman's grip. "Wouldn't you like me to open the curtains? I'm sure you'd feel much better just for being able to see outside and having some light in here."

"That's a wonderful idea. You see, Richard, she's only just arrived and she already knows just what to do."

Elizabeth busied herself pulling back the heavy curtains and looping the ties over their hooks in the window frame. What was it about the Bartletts' manner that disturbed her so?

No question about her being welcome. They seemed happy enough to have her there. More than happy, almost giddy. Maybe that was what jarred. She remembered the Bartletts as somber, rather dour people. This exuberance seemed completely at odds with the people of her memory. She gave the curtains one last twitch and turned back to the bed.

"What an improvement! I feel better already. Come sit beside me, where I can look at you." Letitia's scrawny hand patted at the coverlet.

Elizabeth took a closer look at her patient, viewing the

woman's sallow complexion with concern. She seated herself on the edge of the bed, trying not to flinch when Letitia's waxy hand grabbed at hers.

The afternoon light showed the injured woman's features in unforgiving detail. Limp, graying hair straggled along her cheeks and fell in a tangled mass around her shoulders. The deep vertical lines etched between her eyebrows revealed the woman Elizabeth remembered, confirmed by the fine lines radiating from her lips. This was a mouth more often pursed in disapproval than relaxed in good humor.

Letitia narrowed her pale blue eyes and studied Elizabeth for several moments. Then she patted Elizabeth's hand, and her thin lips stretched in a smile.

Elizabeth returned her scrutiny. The notion struck her that she had entered an animal's den and was about to be devoured.

What a foolish fancy! Elizabeth pressed her fingers to her temples. She must be even more tired than she thought to harbor such uncharitable thoughts about an unwell woman.

"You must be exhausted." Letitia's syrupy voice echoed her thoughts. "Why don't you go lie down for awhile?"

"An excellent idea," Richard said. "Time enough to unpack and get settled after you've rested a bit."

"But. . .I'm here to take care of Mrs. Bartlett, not the other way around."

"Nonsense. We can't have you falling ill before you even get started. Now go along and get some rest. We insist, don't we, Dear?"

"Absolutely. A lovely girl like you needs to take care to maintain her appearance. Once word of your arrival gets out, suitors will be lining up outside our door."

Elizabeth ignored the implied compliment and plumped up Letitia's pillows. "If you have any concerns about my motive for coming out here, let me assure you that finding a husband is the farthest thing from my mind. I have no intention of entertaining suitors."

She eased Letitia back onto the pillows and went to her room, where she found her trunk had already been delivered. She unpacked in short order. Her dresses would need ironing before they were fit to wear, but she could deal with that later.

The two leather bags in the bottom of her trunk, however, did require immediate attention. She lifted the sacks out one at a time, noting that the tie string on one of them was loose. She knotted it tight. She hadn't brought her inheritance money clear across the country to lose it now.

She found Richard in his study. "I need to set up a banking account," she told him. "Could you tell me where the nearest bank is?"

"I'm afraid we don't have one yet." He slid open the bottom drawer of his desk. "But I can keep your valuables in my strongbox, if you like."

"Thank you." She smiled. "It will be a great relief to know it's secure."

Bringing the bags from her room, she watched him put her money inside the strongbox, then lock it and return the key to his pocket. She heaved a sigh of relief and turned to go. Time now to return to Letitia and get on with the job she had come west to do.

"Back so soon?" Letitia's eyebrows arched high on her forehead. "Why, you've barely had enough time to close your eyes, let alone put your things in order."

"On the contrary, I've unpacked and found a place for everything. I'm ready to get to work. What would you like me to do first?"

Letitia gaped at her. "My dear, you must have traveled light. When is the rest of your luggage coming?"

Elizabeth straightened the clutter of tiny bottles on Letitia's vanity table. There isn't anymore. I brought everything I thought I'd need with me." She swiped a dust cloth across the tabletop. The dust swirled and settled in time with her movements.

"It's so dry here, compared to Philadelphia. You'll have to dampen the cloth to catch the dust. But Richard said you had only a carpetbag and one small trunk. Do you mean to tell me that's all you brought? No party frocks? No ball gowns?"

Elizabeth smiled and shook her head. "Don't you worry a bit, Mrs. Bartlett. I'm here to take care of you. Being a part of the local fashionable society doesn't hold a bit of interest for me."

Lifting the pitcher from the washstand, she poured a small amount of water onto the dust rag and worked it through the cloth with her hand. Letitia was right; the dust clung to the cloth and the walnut surface began to gleam.

four

Can I get you anything else?" Elizabeth lifted an empty serving bowl and scooped up a basket of leftover rolls with her free hand.

"I could use some more coffee," Richard said. "Bring a cup for yourself and join us."

"Yes," Letitia said. "You're not a servant, you know. You're a member of the household."

Elizabeth carried the coffeepot and an extra cup to the small table she had set up in Letitia's room. Having the couple share meals together in a more normal setting, she reasoned, might boost Letitia's spirits and hasten her recovery.

After a week, signs of improvement were evident. Already a faint bloom of color had appeared in Letitia's sallow cheeks, and her strength increased by the day. Dr. Warren had been most pleased with her progress on his last visit. The next step in Elizabeth's plan was to coax her charge to take a few steps across the room and perhaps spend some time sitting up in the platform rocker. Maybe this would be a good day to try.

She poured coffee for the three of them and continued to plan her strategy.

Richard's voice interrupted her thoughts. "You're certainly quiet today."

"She's probably thinking about all the friends she left behind," Letitia said, giving Elizabeth a probing look.

"On the contrary. I'm enjoying my stay here immensely."

Letitia simpered. Again, Elizabeth wondered at the smile, so at odds with the lines time had imprinted on her face.

"Even so," Letitia pressed, "there must be someone you miss. A special young man, perhaps? Your coming out here must have left many of them brokenhearted."

Elizabeth stood and began gathering the cups and saucers. "Let me assure you, I am quite content to be here on my own. The men back home are more than capable of carrying on in my absence."

"That's their loss, then." Richard leaned back in his chair and loosened the bottom button on his waistcoat. "Our western men won't be so slow to appreciate your spirit and finer qualities."

"To be sure." Letitia bobbed her head in agreement. "There is any number of young men who would be most anxious to meet you. But you must let us introduce you to the right ones. With your looks and family background, you're sure to receive a worthy proposal in a matter of weeks." For the first time, Elizabeth saw a spark of excitement light her face.

Elizabeth lifted the armload of dirty dishes and turned toward the door. "You don't have to worry about finding suitable prospects for me. Marriage is the last thing on my mind."

A choking sound made her pivot back toward the bed. "You can't mean that." The color in Letitia's cheeks ebbed away, leaving them an ashen gray.

Elizabeth set the dishes down and hurried to the bedside. "Are you feeling unwell? Do I need to call the doctor?"

Letitia waved her away. "I was startled by what you said, that's all." She fixed Elizabeth with a piercing gaze. "You didn't mean that, of course. About having no interest in marriage."

Elizabeth studied the other woman's pasty complexion. If one offhand comment had that effect on her, what would hearing the whole truth do?

She shot a quick glance at Richard. He looked as discomfited as his wife. She wavered, then made her decision. Better to get it all out in the open as soon as possible.

She folded her hands in front of her and drew a deep breath. "My reason for choosing to come out here was not because I had limited prospects at home. I had no interest in attracting suitors then; I have none now. My focus lies in quite another direction."

"And what might that be?" Richard asked, his voice taut.

"To seek my own way as an individual rather than as an appendage attached to a successful man. I want to achieve success on my own. I have no need to divert my energies hunting for a husband."

"That's outrageous!" Richard's indignant sputter brought her explanation to an abrupt halt. "The very idea of a woman striking out on her own!"

"Indeed," Letitia put in. "God made woman to be man's helpmate. A woman isn't complete without a husband."

"Not at all. That may have been the case in years past, but look what women have accomplished just in this century. Why, only last year the American Equal Rights Association was founded for the express purpose of assuring the rights of all citizens regardless of their race, color, or sex."

Letitia stared, her face twisted into its more accustomed scowl. "Rights? What are you talking about? You're beginning to sound like one of those wicked suffragists. I can't believe I'm hearing such things from your lips, Elizabeth Simmons. I'm sure your mother never subscribed to a view like that."

"My mother and I have never seen eye to eye on the topic," Elizabeth admitted. "But that doesn't make my opinion any less—"

"That will be quite enough out of you, young lady." Richard's tone brooked no response. "I cannot control the thoughts you allow to infect your mind, but you had better remember you are here at our invitation. And while you are a guest in this house, I insist you refrain from expressing those sentiments aloud again. Is that clear?"

Letitia punctuated his statement with a firm nod.

Elizabeth stared at them both for a long moment. "Perfectly." She retrieved the coffee service and marched to the kitchen.

The seemingly endless stream of kitchen chores had been put to rest, at least for the moment. Elizabeth pulled her bedroom curtain to one side and took in the view that was becoming more familiar by the day: miners and muleskinners in their rough garb; the better-dressed members of the Territorial Legislature conferring earnestly as they passed along the street. An undercurrent of excitement seemed to pervade every aspect of the new capital. And behind it all, the bulk of Thumb Butte formed a backdrop against the western sky.

One day, as soon as Letitia recovered enough to manage on her own, Elizabeth, too, would be a part of it all.

Recalling Letitia and their heated exchange, Elizabeth tried to set aside her ruffled feelings. Pastor Whitcomb had cautioned her often enough about the dangers of speaking in anger.

Had she done it again? Without a doubt. "I'm sorry, Lord," she whispered, pressing her forehead against the windowpane. "Help me to remember what a wonderful opportunity I've been given. You've provided me with a place to stay and the chance to learn about the possibilities here. Help me to be appreciative and hold my tongue. . .and my temper."

The front door closed with a decisive click. Elizabeth watched Richard descend the porch steps and set off toward the center of town. She followed his progress, wondering if she should apologize for her earlier outburst. She had no intention of changing her opinions, of course, but perhaps she should tone down the way she expressed herself.

❧

"Any mail for me?" Michael scanned the shelves of canned goods, while Nate Smith riffled through the envelopes behind the counter of the general store that doubled as the community post office. Nate separated one letter from the stack and held it up, giving Michael a gap-toothed grin.

Michael took the missive and smiled when he noted the

return address. Amy had responded to his last letter even more quickly than usual. Regardless of their differing opinions on his being in Arizona, he could always count on his sister's steadfast devotion. Nice to know he had at least one family member he could rely on—and to be able to talk to regarding their father's behavior.

He stepped back from the counter and slit the envelope open with his pocketknife. The customer behind him jostled his arm, and he glanced up to see Richard Bartlett staring at him through his spectacles.

The older man's irritated expression turned to one of pleasure. "Ah, Michael. I've been hoping to run into you."

"Excuse me," Michael said. "I have some family business to attend to." He held up the envelope in silent explanation and moved outside into a shadowy corner behind a stack of shipping crates, hoping the maneuver would put him outside Richard's notice.

He slid the thin sheet of stationery out of the envelope and spread it open.

Dearest Brother,

I pray this letter finds you well. And to set your mind at ease, let me assure you right away of my abiding love and support. My questions as to the wisdom of your going to the new territory are due only to my concern for what is best for you. Your description of our father's latest peccadilloes saddens but does not surprise me, these being but one more entry in a long list of misdeeds.

While my love for you never changes, I continue to find myself at a loss to understand your insistence on throwing away your own prospects for a bright future for the sake of a man who not only robbed us of a normal family life but cut short our mother's life, as well.

The rattle of boots rumbled along the boardwalk, and

Michael saw the object of his sister's scorn approaching. Thumbs hooked in his vest pockets, his father held the attention of a small group of men with practiced ease.

Not a group selected from Prescott's finest citizens, Michael noted. What could his father be up to now? He faded back into the shadows and waited. The group stopped just past his place of concealment.

"So you see my dilemma, O'Roarke." The speaker, a florid man with side whiskers, spread his hands wide. "I've submitted my bid to the legislature, but that sanctimonious clerk wouldn't tell me whether I've been undercut by Bauer's crew. I knew if anyone could make sure I get that contract, it would be you." He slid an envelope from his inner pocket into O'Roarke's waiting hand.

Michael's father glanced inside the envelope, smiled, and tucked it away. "That will take care of things nicely. A word in the right ears, and I'm sure I can clear this up for you. Always glad to be of service to a hard-working man like yourself."

"We could use more of your kind in public service," the man said. His companions nodded agreement.

"That's what I like about you, O'Roarke. You always know how to get things done. . .even if it isn't always quite within the confines of the law." The speaker elbowed Michael's father, while the others guffawed.

The knot of men moved on down the street. Michael eased out from behind the crates, swallowing against the taste of bile that rose in his throat. How long did his father think he could sow this kind of corruption before he reaped a harvest of retribution?

He clenched his fists and felt something crackle in his fingers. Amy's letter. He smoothed it out as best he could and tucked it inside the inner pocket of his sack coat. Amy would no doubt classify this as yet another example of their father's unsavory lifestyle. And she would be right. She would also question once again Michael's wisdom in following their father to Arizona.

For the first time, he wondered if Amy could be right on that account as well. Had he made a mistake in thinking his presence might put a damper on their father's shady activities and help bring him to faith in Christ?

Back in Albany, he would have been finishing up the college degree the war had interrupted. He'd be preparing for law school and mapping out his future—and worrying himself sick about his father.

There, he'd be losing sleep wondering what new scheme his father was about to launch. Here, he knew the schemes all too well, but at least he had the chance to be around when his father's misdeeds caught up with him and he finally hit bottom. No getting around it, he needed to be in Prescott.

five

"Won't Mr. Bartlett be surprised when he sees you sitting up on your own?" Elizabeth fluffed one of the bed pillows and slipped it between Letitia's back and the platform rocker. "Are you comfortable?"

"As much as I can be, considering the constant pain I'm in."

Elizabeth bit her tongue and slipped out to the kitchen before she said something she would regret. Letitia had been through an ordeal, no doubt about it. Still, Elizabeth couldn't shake the nagging feeling that Letitia's condition had improved more than she was willing to admit.

She ladled a thick bean soup into a flowered tureen and set it, along with bowls and spoons, on a serving tray. On the bright side, Letitia looked better, even if her attitude showed little improvement.

Elizabeth had spent the morning coaxing Letitia to allow her to wash and dress her hair and helped her change into a housecoat of a soft rose hue that brought a bloom of pink to her cheeks.

She had everything set in place by the time Richard's footsteps sounded on the front porch.

He entered Letitia's room and stopped short when he saw his wife in the chair. The smile that spread over his face gave Elizabeth all the reward she needed. "Wonderful to see you up, my dear." He dropped a kiss on Letitia's forehead and seated himself across from her. "Don't leave just yet, Elizabeth." He pulled a packet of letters from his pocket and handed three to her.

"Three letters!" Letitia gasped. "You must have a host of friends to keep up the steady stream of mail you've been getting."

Elizabeth responded with a brief smile and glanced through

the missives. She recognized her mother's fine script on the first envelope and set it aside. The second was from Carrie.

Guess what event brought Philadelphia's elite to our home last Friday night? None other than Virginia's engagement party!

Elizabeth raised her eyebrows and scanned the letter for the name of her future brother-in-law.

Emerson Fairfield. That figured. Just like Virginia to pick the most solvent of her suitors rather than one with character.

"That's a solemn look," Richard said. "Nothing wrong, I hope."

"It seems my sister, Virginia, has just become engaged to Emerson Fairfield. You may remember him."

Richard sat up straight. "Of the Baltimore Fairfields? She's made a fine match indeed. Your parents must be very happy."

"I'm sure Mother will be thrilled," she replied. She glanced at the second letter. James again. It would be fun to read his take on Virginia's impending nuptials. She started to slit the envelope open, then remembered where she was and turned to go. She would read James's letter back in the kitchen.

"Wait. Why don't you bring another chair and eat with us?" Letitia suggested.

"Of course," Richard said. "No need for you to stay confined to the kitchen like a servant. We've benefited by your help, but we haven't taken time just to sit and chat."

"What a lot of mail you receive!" Letitia gushed when they had all filled their bowls. She cast a sidelong glance at Elizabeth. "You must miss your home very much."

Elizabeth confined herself to a noncommittal murmur.

Apparently misinterpreting this as a sign of agreement, Richard leaned forward, an anxious frown crinkling his forehead. "Perfectly understandable, of course, but you must understand that life out here isn't all drudgery. We're hoping you will extend your stay past the point when Letitia is well again in order for us to prove it to you."

Elizabeth drew a deep breath and patted her lips with her

napkin. "I may as well tell you that once Mrs. Bartlett has recovered, I plan to make my home in Prescott permanently."

Richard and Letitia stared at one another, then looked at her with broad smiles.

"What a wonderful idea," Letitia said. "And there will be plenty of prospects for you to choose from, just you wait and see."

"That isn't exactly what I had in mind."

"Good for you." Richard regarded her with approval. "It's important to be cautious. This is, after all, an untamed territory. We do have our share of riffraff around here."

"Yes, indeed. You can't be too careful." Letitia looked at Richard, her face alight as though she had just come up with a brilliant idea. "And we can help, to repay you for your kindness in taking care of me."

"But I really don't—"

"Of course." Richard picked up on Letitia's thought and forged ahead. "After all, we do know the right people in the territory. We'll help you get acquainted. In fact, I already have an ideal candidate in mind."

Letitia wore a look that reminded Elizabeth of a cat with cream on its whiskers. "We'll have a party—"

"Or perhaps a more intimate dinner—"

"With candlelight and soft music. Maude Avery's son plays the violin—"

"Wait!" Elizabeth planted her palms on the table and pushed herself to her feet, finally bringing the juggernaut to a halt.

"You don't understand." She stared from one of the Bartletts to the other, appalled. "I do plan to stay, but I have no intention of using my time here in pursuit of a husband."

Their looks of astonishment would have been ludicrous if not for the crackle of tension building up in the room. She pushed her chair forward and gripped its back, readying herself to launch into an explanation.

"I want to use my time during Mrs. Bartlett's convalescence

to get to know the area and learn its needs. When the time is right, I plan to launch my own business. At the moment, I'm thinking about dealing in mining supplies. There's certainly a need for them at present and will be for some time to come. Once I'm established, I can expand my inventory as needed."

A long silence followed, broken only by the ticking of the clock on the mantel. Finally, Richard cleared his throat.

"I will speak to you as I would to my own daughter. The business world is no place for a young woman, especially one who comes from such a fine family as yours. I'm certain your parents would never countenance such a thing. Your father is sure to refuse any request for funds to finance such a mad venture."

Elizabeth squeezed the chair back more tightly. "Any number of women have run their own businesses—and quite successfully." She looked out the window and waved her hand at the activity outside. "One reason for my coming to Arizona is that it's new and open and holds such opportunity. And as for needing my father's support, rest assured that I have my own money *and* my father's good wishes. The money I asked you to keep for me is more than enough to open my own business. Its success or failure is up to me."

Letitia pushed herself forward in the rocker. Her eyes held an angry glint. "You're certainly a young woman of strong viewpoints. Unfortunately, propriety dictates—"

"We'll discuss it later," Richard interrupted. "Alone."

The Bartletts continued their meal in stony silence. Elizabeth crumbled a biscuit into her bowl, but the meal she had prepared no longer held any appeal. She set down her spoon, ready to leave.

No. She would not allow them to chase her away from the table as though she were a petulant child. She had done nothing more than express her opinion and outline her plans to them. True, she was a guest in their home, but that didn't mean they could control her thoughts or dictate her future.

She settled back in her chair and pulled Carrie's letter

from her pocket. Typically, Carrie had filled it with news of dinners, balls, and plans for Virginia's wedding. And one wistful comment: *And while all this activity fills my days, I wonder how much of it is of any lasting value. How I wish I could be with you!*

So do I, Carrie dear, so do I. She tucked the letter back in its envelope. The Bartletts maintained their silence, Richard steadfastly ignoring her, Letitia casting quick glances her way from time to time.

James's ebullient personality flowed from his written words as though she could actually hear him speak:

I had a lively discussion with some of the men in my club in regard to women's rights. They thought they had me, until I presented them with some of your arguments. You should have seen how it stopped them cold!

Elizabeth chuckled at the picture his words painted.

"Pleasant news, I trust?" Letitia's voice rasped in the otherwise still room.

Elizabeth grimaced, then forced a smile. "Yes. An amusing story from a dear friend back home." She started to add more but decided to let it go at that.

"Sending letters across the country is not an inexpensive proposition. You must be loved very much to receive such a quantity of mail." The statement came out sounding more like a question, one Elizabeth chose not to answer.

What business was it of the Bartletts' how much mail she received?

six

As a counterpoint to the steadily warming trend in the weather during the days that followed, Letitia's attitude grew increasingly frosty.

"Be more careful with my hair this time. If you keep yanking through it like you did yesterday, I won't have any left."

Elizabeth reached for the porcelain-backed hairbrush and gripped it so tightly the handle bit into her palm. "Such a lovely morning. Would you like me to move your chair so you can see the robins outside?"

"It's no good trying to distract me. Just watch the way you handle that brush."

Elizabeth drew the brush through Letitia's graying locks with gentle strokes and searched through her memory for verses on forbearance. Paul spoke of charity in his first letter to the Corinthians, she remembered. What were some of the characteristics he listed? Oh, yes. According to Paul, charity suffers long and is kind. It bears all things and is not easily provoked.

Paul never met Letitia Bartlett. Elizabeth rebuked herself for the unworthy thought. She would hold her tongue and not respond in kind, however tempting that might be.

Smoothing Letitia's hair into a soft bun, Elizabeth pulled a few strands of hair from the brush and tucked them into the hair receiver on the vanity table.

"Don't think I didn't see that," Letitia snapped. "The way you pull and tug, my poor hair is coming out by the handful."

Teeth clamped together, Elizabeth let herself out of the room and leaned against the wall, fighting for control.

"Difficult morning?"

She whirled to see Richard outlined in the sunlight coming through the kitchen window.

Richard grimaced, and Elizabeth knew she must have failed to keep her irritation from showing.

"You aren't thinking of leaving, are you?"

"Of course not." She tried to ignore her longing to do just that.

Richard took a step toward her, fidgeting with his tie. He glanced at the closed bedroom door and lowered his voice. "I know Letitia is not always an easy person to get along with."

A bear with a toothache might have a sweeter disposition. "Please don't worry. I can manage." She had to. If she let herself be bested by one woman's sour attitude, how could she find the fortitude it would take to make it in the business world out on the frontier?

"I want you to know how much we appreciate everything you're doing."

If he pulls that tie much tighter, he'll choke himself.

Richard took a handkerchief from his coat pocket and mopped his forehead. "Letitia has always been high-strung and tends to have a rather sharp tongue." He paused, seeming to gauge the reaction his words brought. "I'm afraid the accident has only made that worse."

He shook his head, the picture of despair. "I know she hasn't made life pleasant for you lately, and I'm sorry."

You'd better make up your mind whose side you're on. Elizabeth bit back the tart remark. Richard alternated between taking Letitia's part and apologizing for her with a speed that left Elizabeth dizzy.

He went on, his brow creasing. "You've been working too hard. I'm afraid we've taken advantage of your generous nature."

Elizabeth blinked. What could he be leading up to?

"We can't afford to lose you. You need some time off. Starting today, in fact. Why don't I relieve you after lunch, and you can call the rest of the day your own?"

If his wavering attitude kept her off balance, this offer threatened to bowl her over. "That would be. . .very nice. Thank you."

Tension seemed to ebb from Richard's frame. "And if there is anything else that will make your stay more pleasant, you must let me know at once. We couldn't bear the thought of your leaving us." He opened his mouth, then pressed his thin lips together and gave a brief nod. "It's settled, then. I'll be home promptly at lunchtime."

❧

Elizabeth drew in a breath of pine-scented air and reveled in the freedom of this glorious spring day. Although she'd occasionally run a few quick errands for Letitia, she had chafed at not being able to explore the town on her own. This unexpected time off had proved to be more of a boon than Richard could have known.

He had returned as promised and shooed Elizabeth out the door without waiting for his lunch to be served. "I'll see to everything," he promised. "Just enjoy yourself."

What got into him, Lord? The more time she spent around Richard and Letitia, the less she understood them.

No matter. The afternoon was hers to do with as she wished, and she intended to make the most of it.

Freedom beckoned. Elizabeth made her way past the scattered houses until the plaza came into view. She stopped for a moment to take in the scene. Wagons loaded with freight lined up along Gurley Street, awaiting the order to depart. Self-important politicos hurried along the boardwalk, rubbing elbows with dusty miners in town to replenish their supplies. The bustle of a new city trying to discover its identity—much like Elizabeth herself.

A light breeze drifted from the northwest, carrying the scent of fresh-cut lumber from the sawmill. . .a pungent raw smell, full of promise.

If you could capture the excitement and hope of this new land in a fragrance, it would smell like that. Elizabeth filled her lungs with the heady aroma. *This is what God made me for. He brought me out here to be a part of this.* The seed of thought took root and sprang up as a certainty in her heart. "I could stay here forever," she whispered.

She walked to the center of the plaza and pivoted in a slow circle, surveying her surroundings. Where to start? If Richard kept his word and gave her at least one half day a week off, she could make a systematic reconnaissance of the businesses already in place.

Knowing how changeable both Bartletts could be, that might be a pretty big "if." She'd better accomplish as much as possible today.

The saloons of Whiskey Row lined Montezuma Street on the plaza's west side. That eliminated one fourth of the area she needed to investigate. She turned her attention to the buildings on the north side of Gurley Street.

Prescott Market. Blake & Co., Assayers. The Hadley House. The Bowen Mercantile caught her notice; a steady stream of customers entered the clapboard building. Elizabeth saw few women among them, but it didn't matter. What she sought was information. She crossed Gurley Street and pushed open the door.

Inside, a mustachioed man wearing a white apron looked her way.

"Can I help you, Miss?"

Perhaps it would be well to play the part of an ordinary customer rather than a potential competitor. "A packet of pins, please." Elizabeth scanned the shelves for other likely purchases. "And a penny's worth of those horehound drops."

With her reason for being there established, she scanned the faces of the men clustered near the pickle barrel.

"Good afternoon," she ventured. Several of the men nodded; others watched her with guarded expressions.

All right. In for a penny, in for a pound. "I'm thinking of starting a business here. What do you think of Prescott's future prospects?"

The group stared at her as though she had sprouted an extra head. One bearded fellow worked his jaws slowly, then sent a stream of tobacco juice into the sawdust around the cuspidor.

"We've already got a dressmaker," he said, eyeing the pins the proprietor held out to her. "I'm afraid me and the boys won't give you much business that way." His sally brought chuckles from the group.

"You mistake my meaning," Elizabeth retorted. "I'm talking about something more substantial—selling dry goods, perhaps, or mining supplies."

The chuckles grew to outright laughter.

≈

Michael checked off the last item on his freight manifest and pulled the tarpaulin down tight across the wagon box. He turned to the lead driver. "Looks like you're ready, Ben. Keep a sharp eye out for Indians. I want all you boys to make it back safely."

The weathered driver leaned out from the wagon seat and spat in the dust. "I aim to do just that. This trip down to Big Bug may not be a Sunday stroll, but it sure beats that drive in from the river." He wagged his head. "A hundred and eighty miles from La Paz, and only six water holes between there and Date Creek. Dries out a man's bones, just remembering it."

"Well, make this one as quick as you can. I'll see you when you get back." Michael stepped back and lifted his hand to Ben and the drivers of the two wagons behind him. Leather harnesses slapped against mule hides, and the heavy wagons set off.

A small whirlwind spun a column of dust along the street and sent Michael's hat tumbling along the boardwalk. He caught it just past the market and slapped it against his leg to beat out the dust.

The creak of the wagon wheels receded in the distance. His wagons. His business. A business that gave every appearance of growing into a thriving concern. Hard work and fair prices had built a name for the O'Roarke Freight Company, a reputation based on reliability and trust.

Michael knew just how precious that reputation was. He had worked as hard to live down the stigma his father had given to the name O'Roarke as he had to build up the business itself.

A sarsaparilla would go well right now to cut the dust in his throat, he decided. He scanned the length of Gurley Street.

Farther along the block, the door to Bowen Mercantile opened and a woman emerged. Her chestnut curls glinted in the afternoon light as she stood for a moment, then set off in the opposite direction with quick, decisive steps.

For a moment, Michael thought he recognized her, but his memory couldn't supply a name. He squinted against the sun's glare. No, she was no one he knew. But she'd just come out of the mercantile. Someone there might know her.

A wave of laughter trailed off when he pushed through the door. "A bottle of sarsaparilla, please," he said, then turned to the chuckling men.

"Everett been telling more of his stories?"

"Not this time." Roy Guthrie wiped tears of mirth from the corners of his eyes with a frayed bandanna. "He didn't have to. That eastern gal gave us plenty to laugh about without any help from him."

"Eastern gal?" Michael took the sarsaparilla, tossed a coin on the counter, and took a long pull from the bottle.

"The one who skedaddled out of here like Jael getting in the mood to smite Sisera. You must have just missed her."

"She sure didn't miss Everett," put in Harry Goldberg.

"What do you mean?" For the first time, Michael realized Everett was busy mopping himself dry with an empty burlap sack.

Roy grinned broadly. "She came waltzing in here telling us she 'planned to go in business for herself.'" His voice rose to a falsetto pitch, mimicking her tone. "When we tried to guess what kind of business she was after, she said she wanted to sell mining supplies. Can you beat that?"

"So where does Everett come in?"

Roy raised his hand to quell the rumble of laughter. "We thought that was pretty funny, but Everett's the one who told her how to make her fortune."

Michael fixed Everett with a dubious gaze. "Which was?"

Everett gave his face a final scrub with the coarse sack and looked up with a wounded expression. "All I said was, 'If you were sellin' kisses, we'd each buy a hundred.'"

"That's when she grabbed a tin cup from the counter and doused him with pickle juice," Roy explained. He let out a whoop that set the tails of his mustache dancing.

Michael grinned as he hunkered down and rubbed the bottom of the bottle back and forth across his knee. "Any idea who she is?"

Roy shot a keen glance his way. "You wouldn't be fixin' to make yourself a target, too, would you?"

"Just curious," Michael said. "I didn't even get a good look at her, remember?"

"Don't know what her name is," Roy told him. "But I seen her before. She's staying over at Bartletts'."

Michael's blooming interest wilted like a fragile flower in the Arizona sun. Richard Bartlett seemed to pop up everywhere he turned lately.

What was it about that couple that set his teeth on edge? He couldn't pin his feelings on anything specific, but he'd sooner trust a rattlesnake than either of those two. They were on a par with his father, the type who hurried out to the new territory, not to build it into something fine, but to get whatever they could out of it for themselves.

If this chestnut-haired woman was part of that simpering, self-centered crowd with its pompous ways, she held no interest for him at all.

seven

"Where have you been? I can't imagine what you could have found to do that kept you out so long."

"Now, Letitia, I told you she would be gone for the afternoon." Richard gave his wife a consoling pat and shot a furtive glance at Elizabeth. "Remember, we want her to be happy here."

Elizabeth clamped her tongue between her teeth. What a contrast to the sense of freedom she had felt during the past few hours. Already she felt like she'd stepped back into a cage.

Charity suffereth long. It couldn't be easy for Letitia, bound to her bed and chair for weeks on end. Small wonder her temper flared.

"I'm back now. I'll get a fresh nightgown ready and start heating water for your bath."

"Just a moment." Richard's voice stopped her. "I picked up the mail on my way home at noon. This letter is yours. I forgot to give it to you earlier."

Elizabeth accepted it gladly. Spying Carrie's handwriting, she tore the envelope open, eager for news from home. Her sister's girlish chatter about Virginia's wedding preparations would be just the thing to counteract the sour taste left in her mouth by Letitia's greeting.

Are you sitting down, Elizabeth? Papa would have written himself, but he's spending every minute down at his office, and Mama is busy having yet another attack of the vapors. I don't understand all the ins and outs of the situation, but it seems some of Papa's business investments have gone sour, and we find ourselves on the brink of financial disaster. "In serious straits," Papa calls it, although Mama claims we are on the verge of poverty. You should be here to see the uproar!

Virginia storms through the house bemoaning our state in the most dramatic fashion. Not out of concern for Mama and Papa, I'm afraid, but for fear this will hinder her plans for the wedding of the century. Or—horror of horrors!—cause Emerson to reconsider his proposal entirely.

As for me, dear Elizabeth, I am sure my attitude disappoints Mama very much. Instead of feeling we're going through a great tragedy, I have a tremendous sense of anticipation about what lies ahead. All my life, I've heard Pastor Whitcomb assure us that God is able to supply our needs, no matter what the circumstance. And now I shall experience the truth of that statement firsthand. I no longer have to sit and moon about the excitement I've missed by not being with you. I'm having my very own adventure, right here at home! Papa sends his warmest regards. He is so glad you have money of your own so you don't have to worry.

With all my love,
Carrie

P.S. Papa has said I may come to work for him as a secretary. It will save him some money, and I may need those skills to help provide some income if things don't turn around soon. Needless to say, I am delighted, and poor Mama is utterly scandalized.

The letter slipped from Elizabeth's fingers. The room receded and instead she saw the image of Carrie's laughing face. Papa's business in ruins? Impossible! And yet, she knew Carrie wouldn't exaggerate. How could this have happened? More to the point, what should she do?

"Are you going to stand there staring into space or take care of me?" The harsh voice snapped her back to the present.

"Letitia." Richard's voice held a pleading note.

"She's quite right." Elizabeth stood and pocketed the letter. "I've had my free afternoon. It's time I got back to work."

She set her mind on straightening the bed sheets and fluffing the pillows. All the while, her mind whirled with the question of what she ought to do.

She could take the next stagecoach and return to Philadelphia. The thought curdled her stomach, but it had to be faced. Her family needed her.

She smoothed a wrinkle from Letitia's blanket, turning the possibilities over in her mind. If she did go back, would she be a help or a liability? Perhaps it made it easier on them to have one less mouth to feed.

Then there was Emerson. She cringed at the thought of the effect the news of his future bride's impending poverty would have on the Fairfield family. They cared about their money and prestige almost as much as Virginia did.

No doubt he would be too embarrassed to break things off with Virginia now that their engagement had been formally announced. But he'd also be mortified for his fiancée to come from an impoverished family.

She nodded, satisfied that Emerson would do everything in his power to see that the Simmons family's fortunes were restored as quickly as possible.

She poured fresh water into Letitia's tumbler, a little guilty at the relief she felt at knowing she didn't have to leave. But this, too, could be of benefit to her family.

Once her business started making a profit, she would be in the delightful position of being able to send money back to help out. Then both Mother and Virginia would have to admit her initiative was something to be appreciated.

And you'll have to ask forgiveness for your insufferable pride.

That thought tempered her elation somewhat. A woman had an obligation to use the gifts God gave her. She remained convinced of that. How did one do that and still not be prideful about it? There must be a balance; how could she find it?

ॐ

"Back again, are you, Miss Simmons?" Jake Bowen, proprietor

of Bowen Mercantile, shoved his glasses farther up the bridge of his nose and scratched his bald pate.

"I'm afraid so. Are you getting tired of my visits?"

"Not in the least. I enjoy a lady who's as much a pleasure to look at as she is to argue with." His cherubic smile took away any offense his words might have caused. "You've got one of the best minds in the territory, I reckon. Even if everyone else around here doesn't see it that way."

Elizabeth stopped in the act of examining a bolt of printed muslin and forced herself to take a calming breath. Mr. Bowen couldn't be blamed for the opinions of the unenlightened. And she shouldn't be surprised that some people objected to her outspoken views. On the other hand, she didn't have to like it.

"So what do you think of my plan to supply equipment to the miners?"

"Appears to me your idea is a good one. Mining's the magnet that draws people to Prescott, but it's the merchants selling to 'em that makes the real money."

"That's my reasoning exactly." Elizabeth basked in a warm glow of gratification. "There's a lot of call for mining supplies right now. I can start out stocking those and expand my inventory as I become more established. I don't have any plans to encroach on your territory of handling general merchandise, though," she added with a grin.

Bowen chuckled. "You've got a good head on your shoulders, all right." He peered at her over his eyeglasses. "I didn't say it."

"Say what?"

"For a woman. That was what you were expectin', wasn't it? For a minute there, you got all fluffed up like a hen ready to protect her chicks."

Elizabeth drew herself up and lifted her chin. "Surely not." She caught sight of her reflection in the window and laughed. "Well, perhaps you have a point. But have no fear, Mr. Bowen. In my mind, you are definitely on the side of the angels."

She turned at the sound of the door opening and groaned when Harry Goldberg and Everett Watson walked in. Two who were most definitely not on the angelic side of the ledger. Another man entered behind them and stood off to one side.

"Look who's here." Everett sauntered toward her. "That pickle-juice-slinging female who thinks she's going to be a businessman."

Elizabeth narrowed her eyes. She would not be intimidated by the likes of Everett Watson. "God gave women minds, just as surely as He gave them to men. In contrast to you, however, I intend to use the one He blessed me with."

She held her skirts aside and swept past the dumbfounded man as his companion burst into laughter.

"She got you good," Harry sputtered. "She didn't even need any pickle juice this time."

Too incensed to make any further reply, Elizabeth pushed her way toward the door. The third man stood nearby, regarding her with a broad smile.

Elizabeth jerked to a halt in front of him. "And I suppose you're another one who thinks a woman's place is confined to the cookstove?"

The dark-haired man shook his head. "If I had presumed to hold such an opinion before, I would certainly change it now. You most definitely have a quick mind."

Elizabeth waited for him to add "and a lively tongue." When he didn't, she eyed him closely to see if he was making fun of her. Every line of his face showed sincerity—and could that be a hint of admiration?

Her face flamed with embarrassment at her impulsive speech. "My apologies, Sir. It seems I leaped to a totally unfounded conclusion." She looked back at the other two men. "I've seen so much of a different attitude lately, I'm afraid I assumed the worst."

The heat in her cheeks told her she must be as red-faced as Everett. She extended her hand. "I am Elizabeth Simmons.

It's a pleasure to make the acquaintance of one of the few men out here who is able to see a woman as a person of worth in her own right."

⪧

She had a firm, confident grip. Not surprising, after the scene he'd just witnessed. Michael caught himself before the smile that threatened to spread across his face could surface. He had a feeling she'd never believe he was laughing at her victims and not her.

"I'm Michael O'Roarke." He released her fingers reluctantly, missing the contact with her soft skin as soon as she withdrew her hand.

So this was the woman who had bested Everett once before. Michael took his first close look at the mass of chestnut curls framing her oval face. The top of her head didn't come any higher than his nose. He'd seen children taller than that.

But that fiery spirit didn't belong in a child's body. She had dressed Everett down in no uncertain manner. He wouldn't have believed it, had he not seen it with his own eyes. How could so much explosive power be packed into such a small package? Being around Elizabeth Simmons could prove as dangerous as juggling a twenty-pound keg of black powder.

But Michael had a feeling it would be a lot more fun.

eight

Richard poked his head into Letitia's room, where Elizabeth sat reading to her. "I've brought some friends home. Make some coffee and bring it to the parlor. And some of those sweet rolls you made last night."

Elizabeth started at his peremptory tone and glanced at Letitia, who took the interruption with surprising grace. "Go along," she said. "It's some of his political cronies. You'll find that more business is often done in gatherings like this than in official meetings.

"Go on," she urged when Elizabeth hesitated. "It's a fine opportunity to meet some of the right people. Connections like this will be important to you, since you plan to stay on."

Elizabeth moved to the kitchen, pausing in the parlor doorway long enough to count the guests. Five men besides Richard filed in through the front door.

He could have given me some warning. She filled the coffeepot and stirred up the fire in the cookstove, then searched through the cupboards for something suitable to serve as refreshments.

Only a few of the rolls remained. She cut them into halves to make it look like more. Hardly a lavish repast, but it would have to do.

It could have been worse. At least he didn't show up and demand supper for all those men. She carried in the tray of rolls, then went back for the coffee service.

"Pour for us, would you, Elizabeth?" Richard tossed the request out with a casual air.

"Of course." She filled six cups with the dark, steaming liquid, using the time to inspect Richard's guests more closely.

Opposites might attract in some circumstances, but Richard's cronies looked to be men of his own type. Their physical attributes differed, but each one had the appearance of a man totally focused on himself.

"If they'd just listen to me, we could solve this issue in two minutes."

"McCormick's still shaken by his wife's death. He isn't in a mood to listen to anyone right now."

"Maybe we need a new governor, have you thought about that?"

Elizabeth handed out five cups of coffee and looked at the one left over on her tray. Surely she had seen six men enter the room?

Movement from the far corner caught her attention. The sixth man stood in the shadows, observing the goings-on with casual interest, but taking no part in it himself.

With one of his thumbs hooked in a pocket of his vest, he used the fingers of his other hand to preen his enormous handlebar mustache with slow, deliberate strokes.

His gaze fastened on Elizabeth. She picked up the last cup to carry it to him, then set it back on the tray. Something about the way he watched her brought gooseflesh up on her arms. He could come get his own coffee, if he were so inclined.

"I have something here, if you'd care to touch up your coffee a bit." Richard produced a bottle half filled with amber liquid.

Elizabeth wrinkled her nose. With her duties as hostess completed, there was no reason for her to remain. She turned to go back to Letitia.

"Stay here, Elizabeth. We may need you for something."

She shot a startled glance at Richard. Stay in the room with five strange men? Feeling like a fly in a spider's web, she moved to the farthest corner of the room and stood quietly, hands clasped in front of her.

The low murmur of conversation resumed, although several of the men glanced her way from time to time. Elizabeth began to feel like an exhibit on display and disliked the sensation heartily.

A narrow-faced man set his cup down in its saucer with a clank that made her wince. "Where's that bottle, Richard?" he slurred. "I hate wasting good bourbon like that. Get me a glass, and I'll drink it straight."

"Elizabeth! Mr. Matthews needs a shot glass." The slur in Richard's own voice alerted her to the likelihood that he'd started drinking well before coming home.

"They're in the sideboard," she stated, making no move to fetch one. She might have to stay in the room as a courtesy to her host; she did not have to contribute to his guests' debauchery.

Richard sent a furious look her way but relaxed when the other men laughed. "Over here," he told them, pulling out a glass for each one. "Let's wet our whistles with something that hasn't been diluted by coffee."

Elizabeth shrank back against the wall, wishing she had chosen a station closer to the door. To leave now, she would have to cross the room, right past the drinking men.

What about the door to Richard's study? She quickly gave up that idea when she remembered the lone man standing in front of it. Elizabeth darted a glance at him in spite of herself and stifled a cry when she found him staring straight at her.

He didn't flinch at her scrutiny but continued to study her with an intensity that made her skin crawl.

"Sure a pretty one you've got helping out," called Matthews.

"I'll say." A tall, thin-faced man favored her with a loose-lipped leer. "We need more like that around this town."

Richard only tipped a glass of bourbon down his throat. "I'll have to agree that there's a shortage of eligible young ladies in the capital." He looked at the man in the corner and raised his eyebrows questioningly.

The man in the shadows met Richard's gaze, then turned his attention to Elizabeth. Once more she had the feeling of being under inspection. Without making eye contact with her again, the man looked back at Richard and gave him a slow nod that chilled her.

Someone brushed her elbow, and she jumped. Matthews stood only inches from her.

"A real looker, that's what you are." He bobbed his head up and down, a move that threatened to upset his already precarious balance.

Elizabeth moved away, wishing she could disappear.

"Yessir, once the word gets out, every young buck in the territory will be lining up to meet you. Better get all the work out of her you can now," he called across the room to Richard. "This one'll be married off before you know it."

"Enough!"

Her outburst shocked the gathering into silence. Elizabeth felt as stunned as the rest looked. Still, she had their attention; she might as well speak her mind before she lost her nerve.

"Since my future seems to be of such great interest to all of you, let me make one thing perfectly clear. I have no intention of marrying just to assure myself of security. I plan to make my own future."

The two men closest to her chuckled indulgently. Another laughed out loud.

Richard's expression held all the friendliness of a thundercloud. "That will be all from you."

Elizabeth raked him with a scathing look. "I'll be with Mrs. Bartlett if you need me."

❧

"Richard told me of your behavior this afternoon." Letitia pushed away her pie plate and set her fork down with fingers that trembled. "You owe an apology to him, not to mention all the other gentlemen you offended with your rudeness."

Elizabeth felt her back grow rigid. "Not a one of them deserves to be called a gentleman, much less merits an apology."

"We've heard quite enough out of you today, young lady."

Two helpings of venison stew plus a large slice of dried apple pie had toned down Richard's tipsiness somewhat.

He hadn't begun to hear all she had on her mind. "I don't intend to allow a crowd of half-drunken boors to discuss my life."

"Yes, you made your opinions quite clear. And managed to offend some of the territory's most influential men in the process."

"I'm sorry you feel I've been rude to guests in your home. At the same time, their remarks were inappropriate. It is certainly none of their business what my plans for marriage—or lack of them—might be."

The Bartletts exchanged startled looks. "You spoke in haste," Richard said in an appeasing tone. "I can understand that some of their comments might have caused you to say things you didn't mean."

"On the contrary. I meant every word."

"Nonsense," Letitia snapped. "No young woman in her right mind chooses to be a spinster. It isn't respectable."

"Quite right. You have plenty of drive and resourcefulness ,and those are fine qualities, in their place. But it's time you started thinking about settling down. You don't want to focus all your energies on a daydream, only to wake up one day and find out it's too late to have a normal life."

"And we can help." Letitia had dropped her waspish mood and now seemed positively eager. "We'd be happy to introduce you to a young acquaintance of ours."

Elizabeth hesitated, bewildered by the abrupt change in Letitia's demeanor. "Please try to understand. I believe a woman ought to be more than mere decoration. I don't discount the idea of marriage, but I know I possess intelligence and abilities. If I do marry someday, I want to be more to my husband than someone to cook his meals, wash his clothes, and warm his bed."

Letitia's gasp cut off the rest of her intended statement.

Richard's face darkened. "I will not sit here and listen to this," he thundered. "You have much to learn about propriety." He tossed his napkin on the table and stalked out of the room.

Elizabeth cleared away the supper dishes in silence and returned to help Letitia prepare for bed. Letitia raised her arms and waited for Elizabeth to slide the cotton nightgown over her head.

"You've upset Mr. Bartlett quite badly."

What about the way he and his guests treated me? "That wasn't my intention. But I do hold strong opinions about what women are capable of and feel I have the right to express them."

"You might want to think less of your rights and more of your obligations." Letitia scooted back on her bed and settled against the pillows. "Remember whom you have to thank for bringing you out here." She didn't wait until Elizabeth had exited the room before blowing out her light.

Elizabeth pulled the bedroom door closed with a soft click instead of the slam she longed to give it.

nine

Michael whistled as he strode beneath a row of piñon pines along Granite Creek. A freshly signed freighting contract crackled in his pocket. If business continued to pick up at this pace, everyone in Prescott would soon know the O'Roarke Freight Company was the best freight line around. Assuming he could control his drivers long enough to keep his wagons moving.

His happy mood faded at the memory of Walt Logan's disappearance. . .and where he had finally located him. He understood the loneliness men experienced on the frontier, where they outnumbered the women twenty to one. But he could never comprehend the need to seek comfort in the arms of fallen women.

Ben, his lead driver, shared his opinion. But they parted company over Ben's opinion that the women were to blame for the situation. Michael agreed that what they did was wrong, but his heart ached at the idea that many saw that kind of life as their only means of survival. More than one woman left on her own had felt reduced to selling herself to stay alive. He'd like to kick the stuffing out of the men who trafficked in such trade.

He stopped in the shade of a large pine and mopped his brow. The weather had turned warm again after a brief cold snap, but that was typical of weather in this mountain capital. It could just as easily snow again before summer settled in to stay.

From his vantage point on the high bank, he watched the water trickle along the creek bed. He scooped up a handful of pebbles and tossed them into the water one by one. A lovely spot, this, if one could forget what went on in some of the buildings only a stone's throw away.

A woman's high-pitched shriek shattered the idyllic silence. Michael spun around, trying to pinpoint its location.

Another piercing cry. He sprinted toward the source of the sound.

Voices rose on the far side of a row of small buildings. Michael rounded the corner at a dead run and saw a couple entwined at the end of the row. He put on a burst of speed.

In the moment before he reached them, he realized two things: The woman's screams were punctuated by giggles. And the man who held her in his arms was his father.

Dust and gravel sprayed from under his boot heels when he skidded to a halt.

"Indians chasing you?" His father regarded him with a look of cool amusement.

Michael stared from his father to the painted woman at his side, unable to speak a word.

"Cat got your tongue? Allow me to introduce you to Ruby, one of Prescott's most delightful young women. Ruby, my son, Michael."

The woman wrapped one arm around his father's ample waist and gave Michael a broad wink. "I see the resemblance."

"Don't go getting your hopes up, Honey. Michael doesn't indulge."

"That's a pity." Ruby's rouge-coated lower lip protruded in a pout.

Michael looked at his father in disbelief. "I thought you had at least enough decency not to carry on your affairs in public."

"Not so very public." His father looked around at the deserted alley and the creek beyond. "Not until you came charging up, anyway. Speaking of that, what brings you back this way? A sudden decline in your scruples, perhaps? Or maybe you're more like me than you've let on."

Ruby giggled and gave Michael a speculative grin.

Michael ignored her and looked straight at his incorrigible parent. "We need to talk. Now."

His father gave an exaggerated sigh. "I can see things aren't going to work out today, Ruby dear. Run along for now. I'll see you soon."

Ruby trailed her hand along his cheek and turned to go. His father stared after her, turned to face Michael.

"All right, what do you have to say that can't wait?"

Righteous anger exploded in Michael's brain. "I can't believe you've sunk so low." Couldn't he? His father hadn't earned his reputation as a womanizer from idle gossip. But seeing it first-hand made him sick.

"Nothing to get all excited about, my boy. Just letting off a little steam. You wouldn't want to begrudge me that, would you?"

What Michael wanted most at that moment was to grab his father by his jacket collar and fling him down the steep bank of Granite Creek. A good dousing in the icy water might be just what he needed.

"And wipe that sour look off your face. It isn't as if I'm planning to make her your stepmother. She's good for a bit of fun, that's all."

"Good? You don't even know the meaning of the word."

"Where's that Christian charity I hear you harping about so much?" His father roared with laughter at Michael's shocked silence, then moved toward him and draped his arm over Michael's shoulder.

"Come walk with me, Son. I've been meaning to speak to you. This is as good a time as any. I won't mince words, Michael. You need a wife. You've put it off long enough, but it's time you got married. Past time."

Michael twisted to one side and flung his father's arm off his shoulder. "How can you speak to me of marriage when I've just found you behaving like that in broad daylight?"

"Another matter entirely, my boy. You're going to be somebody someday. And I don't mean the owner of a piddling freight business. I haven't spent my life setting the stage for your future to see you throw yourself away on some insignificant enterprise."

"No." Bitterness laced Michael's tone. "You've spent your life focusing on one thing and one thing only: getting whatever you wanted for yourself."

His father pulled a cigar from an inner pocket and took his time trimming and lighting it. He closed his eyes and puffed contentedly before he responded. "I'll grant you it may seem that I've promoted my own interest at times. And I'll admit diversions like little Ruby have been strictly a matter of pleasure. But my political aspirations haven't been only for my benefit. The country is expanding. We're on the edge of the frontier now, but this place won't live in isolation much longer.

"We're building this territory, seeing it start from nothing and shaping it into what it will become. But I'm building something beyond that, Michael. Something for you and me." He blew smoke into the air in a series of quick puffs. "I've sought one thing for years: power. And it's just about within my grasp. I'm talking about a dynasty, Son. A legacy we can share."

Michael stared into his father's keen blue eyes. Eyes so like his own, as was the dark, curly hair. He might be looking at a picture of himself twenty-five years in the future. He prayed the resemblance would only be external.

His anger evaporated, leaving sorrow in its place. "I wish I could make you understand. Your goals are not mine. We're both interested in building this territory, but in vastly different ways. I'm not interested in your brand of wheeling and dealing. I know there's a place in politics for men of God—and heaven knows we need them there—but it isn't the place He's called me to be."

"You fool!" His father spat the half-smoked cigar onto the ground. With one quick thrust of his foot, he sent it flying down the slope and into the creek below. "I didn't raise a man, I raised a simpering fool! Or, rather, your mother did.

It's all the same in the long run." He glared at Michael. "One day, you'll see the truth. I just hope it won't be too late."

❧

"Dear God, how can he believe that web of lies he's spun?" Michael leaned his elbows on his desk and cradled his head in his hands. He didn't remember the walk back to his office, couldn't have told which route he'd taken. He'd returned by pure instinct and holed up like a wounded animal in its den.

Wounded. That's exactly how he felt. His father hadn't dealt him a physical blow, but the result was just as painful. Perhaps more so.

"How have I failed him? Where did I go wrong?" To think that after trying his best to live out the truth of the gospel before his father, the man could still think he'd be willing to drop it all and join him in his power-hungry quest.

His reason for coming to Arizona Territory hadn't been to found a business or make a name for himself. It had been for the sole purpose of shining the light of Christ into the dark corners of his father's life.

And he'd failed. Failed miserably.

Amy had warned him. Before he left Albany and in every letter since, she continued to point out the hopelessness of trying to convince someone who didn't want to be swayed.

When his father ignored all his efforts at first, Michael only dug in and tried harder. Every setback had fueled both Amy's conviction that their father was a lost cause and Michael's determination to prove he wasn't.

Up to now.

What was it Amy had said in her last letter? That their father had robbed them of a normal life? Michael couldn't argue with her there. What about the charge that he'd cut short their mother's life?

A picture of Ruby in his father's arms sprang unbidden to his mind. Michael gasped as though the wind had been knocked out of him.

Could Amy be right? Like a dam had opened, scenes from the past flooded his memory. His gentle, godly mother reading her Bible alone while his father gallivanted off somewhere. Coming across his mother in her sitting room and asking why her cheeks were damp. Seeing her square her shoulders and putting on a brave smile before capturing his attention with some childish diversion.

And once, listening to a conversation between his mother and her best friend. A conversation he wasn't meant to overhear.

"It's happening again, Grace." He remembered the sound of his mother's voice, choked and tight. "I confronted him about it last night. He didn't even bother to deny it, just told me I needn't think he'd let my objections stand in his way. What am I to do?"

Her words had puzzled him at the time. Today, the pieces fell together, revealing the whole ugly picture. How she must have suffered over the years!

Michael clenched his fists. Could Amy be right? Had their father's philandering cost them precious years of their mother's presence?

He had always defended his decision to join their father in Arizona by telling Amy he knew it was the right thing to do. Their mother had prayed faithfully for her husband's salvation. He only wanted to finish the job that meant so much to her.

Now he wondered. Maybe Amy had been right all along. Maybe their father had truly reached a point beyond repentance.

And if that were the case, did he have a reason to stay on here?

ten

Gold pans. Shovels. Blasting caps.

Elizabeth nibbled on the end of her pen. Had she missed anything? She went over the list again, trying to think of other items a miner might need.

Picks. Candles.

She put down her pen and surveyed the list once more. A thrill shivered up and down her spine. One day soon, her store would carry the best selection of mining equipment this side of Denver.

Elizabeth wished her father could be with her to share her joy. Years of watching him work had taught her the value of advance planning. He would be as excited as she to watch her dreams take shape.

More questions remained to be answered. Where would be the best location for her new venture? And what would she need in a building? Elizabeth pulled out another sheet of paper and sank into thought.

A knock on the front door roused her. She left her papers spread out across the table and went through the parlor to admit Dr. Warren.

"How is our patient today?" asked the genial man.

"Quite well, in my opinion." Elizabeth swung the door closed and lowered her voice. "Although she still complains of pain and feeling weak."

The doctor snorted. "Letitia Bartlett complains of everything that could possibly be wrong and a great deal that couldn't. I'll just go have a look, shall I?"

"Of course. You don't need me, do you?" He shook his head, and she returned to her planning. Once Letitia no longer needed her help, she could start setting her plans into motion. She picked up her pen and started sketching ideas for a floor plan. It seemed no time at all before Dr. Warren stopped by to take his leave.

"How is she, Doctor?"

"She'll always have a bit of trouble with that arm, but for all that, she's as fit as can be expected."

"When can she start getting up and around?"

"She could have been up for some time now. Don't let her get away with languishing in her bed all day. She needs to be moving. See that she does." He paused in the doorway. "You've done a fine job, Elizabeth. Just don't let her bully you. I can't stand malingerers."

Elizabeth rushed to the sickroom, expecting to find Letitia as elated as she felt. "Dr. Warren told me the news. Isn't it wonderful?"

"The old fool." The corners of Letitia's mouth curved downward accentuating the deep lines in her cheeks. "He can say anything he likes. He doesn't have to live with my pain." She let out a piteous moan and sank back against the pillows.

"Straighten my blanket, Elizabeth. That quack couldn't be bothered."

Elizabeth hesitated. Surely the doctor knew what he was talking about. And the sooner Letitia could manage on her own, the sooner Elizabeth could make her dreams a reality.

She grasped a corner of the blankets and threw them to the end of the bed. Ignoring Letitia's indignant yelp, she helped the older woman into a sitting position and draped her robe around her bony shoulders.

"Let's get you out into the parlor. You'll feel much better once you're sitting up among all your lovely things. Come on, now."

"Have you taken leave of your senses? I need my rest."

"You can rest in the wing chair. I'll bring some pillows to make you more comfortable."

She put her words into action over Letitia's protests and soon had her seated in the parlor.

"Now, isn't that nicer than staring at the same four walls day in and day out?"

With a colorful quilt draped across her knees and a pink flush tingeing her cheeks, Letitia already looked more robust, although Elizabeth thought the flush might be due more to anger than health.

"What am I supposed to do, just sit here all alone?"

"Why don't I bring my papers from the kitchen and work on them here to keep you company?"

"Why ask for my permission? You'll do as you wish, anyway."

Ignoring the jibe, Elizabeth brought out her papers and spread them next to her on the settee. She bent over the rough map she had drawn of the town. Would it be best to locate her store facing the plaza or on one of the outlying roads? She touched different spots with her finger, trying to envision her business in each place.

"You mean you're still bent on pursuing this foolish notion? You'll wake up one day and realize all the good husbands have been taken, mark my words."

"I'm not worried about it." She returned her attention to her map. Perhaps she could find a suitable building already in place. That would save her a good deal of time.

"And think of children. They'll be a comfort in your old age."

"Really, Mrs. Bartlett—"

"Richard and I always wanted a large family, but it was not meant to be, more's the pity."

The front door opened, saving Elizabeth from another onslaught.

"You're up, my dear!" Richard burst into the room.

"Only because she forced me here. That idiot doctor is trying to say I'm fully recovered. You must make him understand that I still have a long way to go."

"Good, good," Richard murmured.

"Good? Richard, do you hear a word I'm saying? I still need Elizabeth's help. You must make him see reason." She glanced at the mantel clock. "What are you doing home so early? It's only the middle of the afternoon."

"Ah, yes." Richard darted a quick glance from his wife to Elizabeth, then back to Letitia again. "Everything's in a bit of a muddle. Mr. Fleury is all stirred up. Some flap about missing money."

Letitia's hands knotted in the folds of her quilt. "And they sent you home?"

"They sent everyone home while he and Alsap go over the books. I'm sure it will come to nothing. More than likely, a clerical error. It's sure to turn up before long."

He beamed and rubbed his hands together. "In the meantime, let's celebrate your progress. With you on the mend, Elizabeth will have time to pursue a social life," he said, emphasizing the last two words.

Letitia's mouth formed an O. "You're right. We were just discussing that, weren't we, Elizabeth? Now we'll be able to pay you back for your kindness and help you meet a fine young man. Doesn't that sound like a good plan, Richard?"

"Yes, and the sooner the better. We've imposed upon her good nature for far too long." He pulled two letters from his coat pocket and glanced at the envelopes. He handed the top one to Letitia. "And this one's for you, Elizabeth."

"Thank you." She accepted the letter without looking at it, not wanting to be sidetracked. "But please don't feel you owe me anything. It was my choice to come out here, and that was to seek out business opportunities, not to enlist you as matchmakers."

She waved her hands as she spoke, and the envelope flew from her fingers, landing on the floor near Letitia's feet. Letitia bent forward and stared down at it, then gave Elizabeth a sharp glance.

"Who spends so much time writing to you? That's the

same handwriting I've seen on several other letters, and I know it isn't your mother's."

It is none of your business who does or doesn't write to me. As Elizabeth scooped up the envelope bearing James's bold scrawl, an idea dawned in her mind. Maybe she could convince them she didn't need to find a beau.

"It's from a dear friend at home," she said brightly. "A gentleman friend."

Their reaction couldn't have been more satisfactory. Letitia gaped; Richard sputtered.

The Bartletts exchanged a long glance. "Is it—"

Richard cleared his throat, interrupting Letitia. "Is it a serious relationship?" he asked. "As your protector while you are away from your father's care, I feel a responsibility for you. What are this man's intentions?"

Elizabeth suppressed a smile. Here was her chance to lay their plans to rest once and for all. "You remember James Reilly, don't you? I can assure you his intentions are entirely honorable." The memory of their childhood pledge popped into her mind. "As a matter of fact," she added with a playful laugh, "he asked me to marry him some time ago."

Letitia's anguished cry echoed through the parlor. Richard's jaw hung slack.

Elizabeth stared at them, mystified. Why should her marriage plans—or lack of them—matter to the Bartletts one way or another? She hadn't expected to shock them so. Still, if that tidbit of information put an end to their scheming, so be it.

"Why didn't you tell us?" Letitia demanded. "You should have let us know you had an understanding with this man, instead of coming to us under false pretenses."

Elizabeth blinked at her. She turned to Richard, hoping for some explanation, but he stood as if frozen, staring across the room. He clutched one hand to his chest, and his face took on a grayish hue.

He looks like he's about to collapse. Dear Lord, what have I done? Elizabeth took a tentative step toward him, but he waved her away and staggered toward the door.

"I must let Timothy know," he called to Letitia, just before the door closed.

Time seemed to stop, while Elizabeth's mind whirled, trying to make some sense of what had just happened. Richard looked terrible, and somehow she felt responsible.

"Do you think he'll be all right? Should I go after him?"

Letitia directed such a malevolent glare at Elizabeth that she held up her hands, as if warding off a physical blow. "Leave him alone. You've done enough."

"But all I said was—"

"You said more than enough. If something does happen to him, it will be your fault. Now take me to my bedroom. I need to lie down."

Elizabeth complied without a word.

⊷

Pale gray light seeped into Elizabeth's room. She had struggled throughout the night to comprehend what she had done to stir up such a hornet's nest, but she was no closer to understanding Richard's strange behavior than before. Her memory of the previous evening remained a blur of catering to Letitia's every whim, then turning out the lights and settling in for the night. Later, the click of the front door marked Richard's return, followed by urgent whispers coming from Letitia's room.

She hadn't even had the energy to light a candle at bedtime, let alone undress. She lowered her feet to the floor and pushed herself upright, feeling as frowsy and rumpled as her clothing.

She had hoped for enlightenment during the long night hours, for clarity of thought that would show her what she'd done. Instead, she only felt confused and resentful at the treatment she had received.

The light grew stronger. Elizabeth reached for her Bible as though grasping a lifeline. Somewhere in its pages, she ought to find some answers. Pastor Whitcomb had been particularly fond of Ephesians. She turned to the spot, her gaze settling on the fourth chapter.

" 'And be ye kind one to another. . .' " *Ha! The Bartletts have shown me anything but kindness.* " '. . .tenderhearted, forgiving one another. . .' " Another area where they fell short. A less tender heart than Letitia Bartlett's would be hard to find.

Forgiving one another. . . Wait a minute, Lord. Am I supposed to hold them blameless for the outrageous way they've treated me?

Maybe one of the Gospels would have the comfort she sought. Matthew, perhaps.

" 'And why beholdest thou the mote that is in thy brother's eye, but considerest not the beam that is in thine own eye?' "

Elizabeth read the passage through twice, then read it again. "No, Lord. It's the other way around. They have the beam; I have the mote."

She flipped through the pages hurriedly. Surely there would be a verse that would shed light on how wrong the Bartletts were.

" 'Obey them that have the rule over you. . . .' " She slammed her Bible shut. The Bartletts didn't rule her life. *No, but they invited you here and let you stay in their home without charge.* But that didn't put them in authority over her, did it?

Didn't it?

"All right, Lord, I wouldn't be here if it weren't for their generosity. This is their home, and I'm only a guest here. I'll try to be more kind, but I'm going to need Your help."

She picked out a clean dress and prepared to fix breakfast.

eleven

Wherefore take unto you the whole armour of God, that ye may be able to withstand in the evil day, and having done all, to stand.

Michael stared at Paul's words to the Ephesians, then slowly closed the leather cover and sat with his hands folded atop his Bible.

He wished the full meaning of the words could somehow seep from the printed page through his fingers, then into his mind. No, his mind understood them all right. He needed to have them imprinted on his heart. He pressed the heels of his hands against his eyes. Hadn't he done everything possible to show his father the value of putting God first in his life? Hadn't he given up prospects for a bright future in Albany for his sake?

And for what? To watch his father pawing a woman of ill repute right out in public? The memory of the scene he'd witnessed sickened him.

No son could have done more than he had. Few would have done as much. He couldn't think of one thing more he could do.

"And having done all, to stand."

Michael spread his arms wide and turned his face toward heaven. "Stand, Lord? Just stand by and watch while he brings more shame to our family?"

His words seemed to bounce back off the ceiling. Silence settled around him like a blanket.

"Why is it so difficult just to stand and watch You work, Lord? I know my limits, know them all too well. It seems a simple enough thing to step back and get out of Your way, but it's harder than it sounds. I guess I never thought of standing firm for my beliefs as being such a passive job."

The memory of Elizabeth Simmons lecturing the men in the mercantile came to mind. Michael chuckled, despite his frustration. Elizabeth's brand of feistiness was far more in line with what he'd always thought of as standing up for one's convictions.

Now there was a woman who knew what she believed and stood ready to defend it. Just the thought of those flashing hazel eyes and all that energy wrapped up in such a petite frame lightened his mood. Under other circumstances, he'd think seriously about paying Miss Elizabeth Simmons a call.

That pleasant image dissolved when he pictured himself climbing the porch steps of the Bartlett house. For the hundredth time, he wondered how such a vibrant woman could be associated with that couple. It didn't make sense.

Michael returned his Bible to its place on the corner of his desk and straightened a stack of invoices. He probably ought to declare Elizabeth strictly out-of-bounds. But he had the uneasy feeling she had already staked a claim in his heart.

❧

"Good morning."

Richard and Letitia looked up when Elizabeth entered the kitchen.

She made her way to the stove, determined to follow the Scriptures and show them kindness. She glanced at her charge while she cracked eggs into a large bowl. Either Richard had helped Letitia with her clothing or she had managed to dress on her own. A quick look at Richard revealed he had regained his normal color, a welcome sight after last night's scare.

Richard slid an unopened envelope across the table to his wife. "It's from Muriel Stephens, back home. I found it on the parlor floor. You never did read it yesterday after. . ."

"After that spectacle Elizabeth put on," Letitia finished for him. She opened the letter without further comment.

Elizabeth opened her mouth to make a retort, then clenched

her teeth and concentrated on whipping the eggs into a frothy mass. While they cooked, she sliced off thick slabs of bread and set out bowls of jelly along with the place settings.

"Be ye kind to one another, tenderhearted." She slid the eggs onto a serving platter and reached for the coffeepot.

Letitia gasped. "Oh, Richard!"

Elizabeth pivoted so quickly that several scalding droplets splashed on her hand. "What is it? Are you ill?" She set the coffeepot on the table and dabbed at her hand with a dish towel.

Letitia waved her hand as if shooing away a fly and shoved the letter at her husband. "Richard, read this." She indicated a point halfway down the page.

Richard's features sharpened as he skimmed the letter, then spread the sheet of paper out and went over the message a second time. He raised his gaze to meet Letitia's.

Elizabeth blew on the spot where the hot drops had spattered on her skin and tried to decipher the unspoken messages that flashed between the couple.

"Is everything all right? Have you had bad news?"

A delighted smile lit Richard's face, to be swiftly replaced by a concerned frown. "Not at all. Not us, that is." He motioned to her chair. "Maybe you'd better sit down."

Letitia reached over and patted her arm. "You poor dear. You'd better tell her, Richard."

Elizabeth gaped at Letitia and felt her knees buckle, dropping her to the chair seat. Had something happened to her family?

Richard held up the letter. "Mrs. Stephens has shared some surprising news. I'm afraid you may find this upsetting." His somber tone didn't match the exultant gleam in his eyes.

"She sends news of several mutual acquaintances," he went on. "Your James Reilly is one of them." He looked her straight in the eye and cleared his throat. "It seems Mr. Reilly has just announced his engagement to Josephine Brown."

Elizabeth waited for stunning news, then realized she

had just heard it. She smiled at the Bartletts, both watching her intently.

"That's wonderful news. Josephine has a mind sharp enough to match wits with James, but a gentle spirit. She'll be a perfect match."

"There, now." Letitia leaned close and put her hand on Elizabeth's. "There's no need for you to put on a brave front."

"Brave front? But—"

"Certainly not," Richard said. "A cad like that doesn't deserve defending."

"I'm not defending him. I—"

"It's all right, Dear. We know you must be heartbroken."

"Heartbroken? Over James?" Elizabeth laughed aloud.

"She's becoming hysterical, Richard. What should we do?"

Still sputtering with laughter, Elizabeth put up her hands to fend off their ministrations. "I'm neither heartbroken nor hysterical. The very idea! Whatever gave you such a notion?" Her mirth faded as she watched their expressions change from sympathy to suspicion.

Richard's eyes narrowed. "It's very odd that you take this so lightly, since he's the one you promised to marry."

"Marry James? Oh!" She remembered her lighthearted comment of the night before and chuckled. "That happened when we were children." She stared with growing concern at their hostile expressions. "What's the matter?"

"What do you mean, when you were children?" Letitia's breath came in ragged gasps.

"It's no great mystery," Elizabeth said with a return of her former spirit. "We grew up next door to each other, as I'm sure you remember."

Richard's face hardened. "But you told us you were engaged to him."

"You may have taken it that way," Elizabeth countered. Her conscience prodded her. Of course they had. Wasn't that exactly what she'd intended?

She sat straighter in her chair and looked squarely at them. While she felt they had brought this on themselves, she knew they deserved an explanation.

"It's all because you were pressing so hard to attach me to someone out here. I thought perhaps I could put a stop to it if you thought I was unavailable. I only said that to—"

"You lied!" Richard slammed his fist on the table, rattling the untouched breakfast dishes.

"Lied!" Letitia echoed. She covered her face with her hands and sank into her chair, loud sobs racking her body. "What are we to do, Richard? Is it too late to talk to Timothy?"

"I don't understand." Elizabeth raised her voice to be heard over Letitia's wails. "I apologize for any misunderstanding, but I fail to see—"

"That's just it." Richard's harsh tone cut across her words. "You don't see at all."

He loomed over her and planted his hands on either side of her against the chair back. Elizabeth shrank back against the unyielding wood. His hot breath puffed against her face. For a moment the world existed only of Letitia's keening and Richard's contorted features.

"We're ruined." Elizabeth could see the veins on his forehead pulse as he ground out the words. "Do you understand? Ruined!"

twelve

Letitia raised her head and looked daggers at Elizabeth. Her hair had escaped from its pins and stringy gray strands dangled on either side of her tear-streaked face. "You haven't been honest with us from the moment you arrived, have you? You wanted a way out here and you used us as a reason to come. We'd planned such a wonderful future for you, but you wanted nothing to do with it. All you've been interested in is following your own desires."

"That isn't true."

"Do you deny that you misled us about your relationship with James Reilly?"

"Misled, yes. Maliciously, no. I only meant to deflect your interest in finding me a beau. I never intended to cause you any harm." Elizabeth stared from one of the distraught pair to the other.

"But just how could my statement about James bring you to ruin? I don't understand."

Richard opened his mouth, then closed it again as he shoved himself away from her chair. Letitia swiped a clump of hair back away from her face and pushed herself to her feet.

"I'll tell you how." Ignoring Richard's cautioning gesture, she declared, "Our money is gone. All of it."

"Financial reversals," Richard put in.

"We had one chance to recoup our losses. Just one."

"An offer from an old and trusted friend."

"His son needs a wife," Letitia said. "All we had to do was produce a suitable candidate—"

"And let nature take its course, so to speak."

"All you had to do was let us introduce you to this young

man. You're attractive enough when you aren't spouting off those idiotic ideas about women's rights. You could have caught his attention if you'd only tried."

"Things move quickly out here," Richard said. "You could have been married before Christmas."

"Married!" Elizabeth heard her voice come out in a squeak.

"All you had to do was agree to meet him. We could have kept things going from there." Letitia's voice rose to a piercing level. "But, no. You couldn't be bothered to show us the least amount of gratitude for bringing you out here, for giving you our protection and a roof over your head. Not the least bit of cooperation. And now it's too late!" The shrill scream echoed through the house, leaving a bitter silence in its wake.

"Too late? Too late for what?"

"For giving us the help we needed, you foolish girl! After you led us to believe you were engaged to James Reilly, Richard went to tell Timothy the deal was off. And now, after you've shattered any hope we had of restoring our fortune, you tell us it was all a lie."

Elizabeth remembered Richard's parting words the night before. She leaned forward in her chair. "Let me get this straight. My meeting this person was going to help you regain your wealth?" A horrible notion struck her. "Do you mean to sit there and tell me you were going to provide me as a wife to this man's son. . .for a price?" She sprang to her feet, quivering with rage.

"All you had to do was—"

"All I had to do was sell myself—no, allow myself to be sold. Isn't that right?" She searched their faces and found confirmation. "My mother worried about my living in the midst of ruffians and cutthroats. When she said that, she had no idea I'd be living under their very roof. This is barbaric!"

"That will do, young lady!" Richard thundered. He pointed a trembling finger straight at Elizabeth's face. "I will not have you speak to either my wife or me with disrespect."

Elizabeth pushed his hand aside. "How dare you speak of disrespect! This country just endured years of war to *end* the abominable practice of people being bought and sold like commodities."

"You can talk, can't you?" Letitia stood and joined Richard. "You've never experienced want a day in your life. You have no idea what it means to have everything stripped away from you, then have one chance to turn it all around again. And then see it snatched away by an arrogant chit of a girl." Her face darkened, then twisted with anger. "Get out! I won't have you in my home another day!"

Elizabeth held her gaze, chest heaving. "Very well. I'll be only too happy to leave this place." Without another word, she swept out of the kitchen.

It took little time to jam her belongings back into her trunk and carpetbag. She set the carpetbag on the front porch, then returned for the trunk. With clenched teeth, she tugged at the handle, dragging it across the floor with a screech she knew would set Letitia's teeth on edge.

Out on the porch, she closed the front door with a bang. After a pause to catch her breath, she picked up her carpetbag and prepared to set out and realized she hadn't the least idea where she should go.

Wagons creaked along the dusty roads. Children called back and forth from neighboring yards. The pound of hammers resounded from building sites. The town teemed with activity, but none of it related to her.

The carpetbag weighed heavy at the end of her arm. She had dreamed of one day leaving this house to venture out on her own, but she'd planned to have a destination in mind when that day arrived.

Perhaps a boardinghouse. Of course. One that accepted ladies. And she had spotted just such a place on one of her jaunts around town. Mrs. Keller's establishment would fit the bill nicely.

She set off toward Cortez Street, the carpetbag bumping against her leg with every step. Surely Mrs. Keller would know someone she could send after the trunk. If not, she would come back and drag it every inch of the way there herself.

Elizabeth strode south on Cortez, revising her carefully laid plans. Her agenda had been to order stock and locate a site before moving out, but she could adjust her plans to compensate.

She would get settled in her new lodgings this morning. If she could inspect the properties she had in mind in the afternoon, she might be able to finalize the purchase of her new property within the week.

She came to an abrupt halt in the middle of the street, bringing a squawk of protest from the driver of a freight wagon.

Her money still rested in Richard's strongbox. The little she carried in her reticule might pay for a few nights' lodging but would hardly serve to strike a business deal.

She had no desire to return to the Bartletts' home. But she had no choice. Turning around, she retraced her steps. She started up the front porch steps, then paused. It would be all too easy for the Bartletts to ignore her knock. Very well, she wouldn't give them the opportunity.

She set the carpetbag down at the foot of the steps and hurried around the house to the kitchen door. Turning the knob, she stepped inside.

Letitia's eyes bulged. "How dare you enter this house without knocking!"

Elizabeth held her ground. "I'm only here to collect the last of my things." She turned to Richard. "The money I gave you for safekeeping. If you'll just get it for me, I'll be on my way."

Both the Bartletts froze. Richard's face darkened, while Letitia turned pale. *Now what?* Whatever response she'd anticipated, she hadn't foreseen anything like this.

Richard's high color faded to a pasty gray. Elizabeth reached out to him, fearing he was about to collapse.

"Pull a chair up behind him, quickly," Letitia ordered. She fluttered next to her husband and helped him into the chair Elizabeth brought.

"Is there anything I can get for him?" Elizabeth asked.

Letitia stood with her hand on Richard's shoulder and faced Elizabeth. "The best thing you can do for either of us is to leave. Right now."

"But my money. If you could just get that for me first—"

"Gone," Richard said in a hollow voice. "All gone. I lost it in a faro game."

"You. . .you lost my money? You gambled it away?"

"Only part of it at first." He stared at a point on the wall across the room. "Thought I could win it back and return it all before you ever knew it was gone. But I hit an unlucky streak. The cards took it all. Every bit of it."

"That money was mine! You stole it. I'm going straight to the sheriff's office."

"It won't do you any good." Richard's eyes had lost their glassy look. "You don't have a receipt for it. It'll be your word against mine."

"But. . .you stole it."

"Don't talk to us about stealing after what you've done." Letitia's voice shook. "You've cost us far more than that. Now get out of this house, and don't come back."

In a daze, Elizabeth returned to the porch for her carpet-bag and headed back to Cortez Street.

❧

"Here I am, Lord, on my own. No one to rely on but myself. And You, of course. That's just what I asked for, isn't it?"

Elizabeth perched gingerly on the narrow bed's thin mattress and surveyed her new domain. The trunk, delivered by Mrs. Keller's handyman, took up most of the floor space. At the foot of the bed, a rickety table held a chipped basin and pitcher. A plain wooden chair sat against the opposite wall under a row of pegs to hold whatever clothing wouldn't fit in the narrow dresser. She would have to leave most of her belongings folded in her trunk.

Elizabeth edged between the bed and the trunk toward the tiny window. Her weight on the floorboards sent the basin and pitcher to vibrating.

"Somehow this isn't quite the way I'd envisioned it, Father. I'm supposed to be conquering new worlds, not hiding out in a cramped little room wondering how I'll manage once my money's gone."

Amazing, the difference twenty-four hours could make. Yesterday she had been happily planning her future. Today she had gone from that to learning she'd been brought out here as merchandise to being cast out, alone and penniless.

Feeling sorry for herself wouldn't do a bit of good. There had to be something she could do, a job of some sort to help her get back on her feet. But what? She thought of the saloons lining Whiskey Row, the last resort of more than one woman left on her own.

No. Never that. She'd starve first.

In better times, she could have written to her father. He wouldn't hesitate to send her money to tide her over. If he had it himself. Which he didn't.

She could appeal to Virginia and her fiancé. The very thought twisted her stomach.

Stop it! There had to be a way, something she wasn't seeing yet. Even Carrie had shown more spirit, looking forward to God's provision like a child who fully expected her Father to live up to His promise.

All right, then. Did she think God's arm was too short to extend to Arizona Territory? She had to shake off this panic and get a grip on her emotions.

She could start by arranging her room. Once she put that small space in order, she'd be in a better frame of mind to plan her next move.

The dresser filled quickly. Elizabeth hung most of her

dresses from the pegs on the wall. She reached into the trunk for her heavy flannel nightgown, then put it back. The nights had been growing warmer, and this room promised to be downright stuffy. Where had she packed her lighter gown?

She found it squashed flat in the bottom of the trunk. No matter. No one would see her wearing it. Something clinked when she pulled it out.

Elizabeth bent to investigate. A gold double eagle nestled against the lining. She remembered having to retie the strings when she pulled the second bag of money out to give to Richard. This piece must have fallen out then. But one wouldn't clink by itself. She pushed aside her clothes and found two more.

The three coins lay in the palm of her hand. Sixty dollars, the remnant of her fortune. Each coin carried the new motto: In God We Trust.

A slow smile spread across Elizabeth's face. "Okay, Lord, it's a start. Let's find out what You're going to do next." She placed the coins in her reticule and descended the narrow stairs.

"I'm going out for a bit, Mrs. Keller."

"Really, Dear, you don't need to check in with me every time you leave." Her landlady's cheerful countenance added to the resurgence of Elizabeth's confidence.

Elizabeth set her face to the north and walked up Cortez, feeling a shiver of anticipation run up her arms. God had promised to provide. He owned the cattle on a thousand hills; the wealth of the universe was His. Surely He could meet the needs of one young woman.

She paused at the corner and waited for a buggy to pass before she crossed Goodwin Street. "We walk by faith and not by sight, Lord," she murmured. "Guide my steps and show me the way."

Hurrying across in the buggy's wake, she stopped again on the opposite corner. A pair of miners hovered nearby, leaning against a loaded wagon.

"If you're sure we've got everything, we can head back to the claim," one said, climbing to the wagon seat.

A spasm of frustration clenched at Elizabeth's stomach. If all had gone according to plan, those same miners would have been her customers, purchasing their goods from her store.

"Guess we've got everything on the list," the second miner replied. He scratched his stomach with a grimy hand. "Only one thing I'd like to have and can't, and that's a cherry pie."

"Or peach pie, or apple pie. Or even an applesauce cake. Old George Bernard makes a mean venison chili, but I haven't had decent baked goods since I left St. Louis." The bearded man shook his head mournfully and climbed up beside his partner. With a shake of the reins, he started their wagon down the street.

Elizabeth stared after them. Baked goods? She'd never considered the need for those before, but she could turn out as fine a pie crust as any baker. Her only domestic accomplishment, her mother called it.

If those miners wanted baked goods, then baked goods she could give them. All she needed were equipment, ingredients, and a place to do her baking.

"I don't have any of those, Lord. What are we going to do about that? Oh, and a place to sell them would be helpful, too."

She proceeded north on Cortez, skirting around a cluster of men standing on the edge of an empty lot.

"You're really pulling out for good, Bill?"

A barrel-chested man nodded. "I came with all these grand ideas of making enough to get a new start, but they've all come to nothing. Guess I'm just not cut out to be a miner. It's time for me to go back to farming and making harnesses."

"Sorry to see that happen," his friend replied. "This would have been a nice place for a saddle shop."

Elizabeth's steps slowed, and she stopped, eavesdropping shamelessly.

"It's yours, if you want it," Bill said. "I just want what I paid for it. That'll get me the rest of what I need to head out."

"Excuse me." The group parted as Elizabeth marched up to the one called Bill. "Did I understand you to say you're selling a piece of property here?"

"This very lot we're standing in front of," he said. "I'm bound for Kansas as soon as I get rid of it."

"How much do you want for it?" She ignored the snickers behind her.

The brawny man grinned. "Lady, I paid forty dollars for this piece when they auctioned the first lots in '64. If I can get that back, I'll be on my way."

Forty dollars. Two-thirds the sum total of her worldly goods.

"Would you accept half now and half later? I'd be happy to have papers drawn up to that effect."

"Twenty dollars now and twenty more by the end of the week, and the place will be yours. Let's go find one of the lawyers here to write up a quitclaim deed."

Two hours later, Elizabeth burst into the boardinghouse. "Mrs. Keller, may I use your oven? And some of your pie pans?"

Mrs. Keller looked up from setting lunch on the table. "I don't see any reason why not." She smiled at Elizabeth's exuberance.

"Bless you! The delivery boy is bringing flour, lard, and dried fruit from the market. I'll get started making pies as soon as I change my dress. I'm going to open a bakery, Mrs. Keller. If I hurry, I just might make my first sale today!"

⁂

"Pies for sale."

The hastily lettered sign hung from a plank stretched across two empty wooden crates. Steam rose from the six apple pies set out on the crude counter.

Elizabeth pulled her handkerchief from her sleeve and dabbed at her forehead. After the breakneck pace of the last few hours, she felt drained. Drained, and yet energized.

She squinted into the late afternoon sun. People strolled

around the plaza. A number of miners were headed for Whiskey Row. In another hour or two, she would know whether she had made a solid business decision or thrown her money away.

"At least this lot is mine. Even if nothing comes of the bakery, I still have enough to pay what I owe on it. I'll have an investment in the property, if nothing else."

"Talking to yourself?"

Elizabeth looked up into a pair of merry blue eyes. "Mr. O'Roarke. Would you like to buy a pie?"

"I was drawn in equal parts by the delectable aroma and the opportunity to talk to the best conversationalist in Arizona Territory. Even if she's already talking to herself." The skin crinkled at the corners of his eyes when he smiled. Elizabeth found herself smiling back.

"As I live and breathe, I did smell apple pie." A man appeared at the edge of Elizabeth's lot and hurried to the makeshift counter. "I'll take this one. No, make it two." He reached in his pocket.

"This one is already taken." Michael scooped up the nearest one. "It looks like business is booming." He gave her a wink that shot a surge of delight right through her.

"Thank you. And you, Sir." Elizabeth beamed at her other customer.

"Is this a onetime sale, or will you be back again?" he asked.

Elizabeth looked at her three remaining pies, then at the group of men heading her way from the plaza. "The Capital Bakery will be open for business tomorrow." She grinned at Michael and squared her shoulders. "And for a long time after that."

thirteen

Elizabeth put up her hand to shield her eyes from the bright noontime sun shining down on the plaza area. Soon, she would have to put up an awning to protect her from its heat. Today, though, the dazzling rays reflected her own sunny mood.

After selling out her entire inventory her first day in business, she had invested her proceeds in more ingredients and some pie tins. She sold out again the following day. And the next, and the next. Capital Bakery had become an overnight success. She had enough to pay Bill Wilson the remainder of what she owed on the lot and some left over besides.

Elizabeth breathed a prayer of thanks and smiled at the customers heading her way. The miners had turned out to be her biggest advertisers, spreading the news about her wares throughout the community.

Elizabeth chuckled. Miners had been her intended customers from the beginning. Only her wares had changed. "You knew it all the time, didn't You, Lord?"

She watched a group of three miners who had just bought a pie together split it into chunks and begin eating. Maybe she could add a few tables and chairs, give them a place to sit, and sell it by the slice. It would make good advertising, as well as more profit.

"A penny for your thoughts."

"Add some more and you can buy a pie. I'm sure it would be tastier than my thoughts."

Michael shook his head. "I'm equally sure it wouldn't. Your thinking is very fresh and just as delightful to the senses." Michael leaned over to savor the aroma of each pie. "But the conversation would be even better accompanied by some of that peach pie."

Elizabeth grinned and handed it to him. "And what would you like to discuss today? The Indian problem, perhaps, or the suffrage issue?"

"I was thinking more along the lines of whether a certain bakery proprietor would like to go with me to C. C. Bean's Bible study."

"It sounds wonderful." Her shoulders drooped. "But I don't see how I can."

"Oh?"

"Mrs. Keller has been wonderful about letting me use her oven, but I can't be in the way when she's cooking for her boarders. The only way I've been able to produce pies in this quantity is to work in the kitchen at night."

Michael let out a low whistle. "I never thought about what you had to do to make this many." His brow wrinkled. "But you're here from late morning on. When do you sleep?"

She gave him a tired smile. "I catch a nap while the last pies are baking, and I rest a little more before I come down here, then try not to think about it the rest of the time." She laced her fingers together and stretched her arms in front of her, then rolled her head from side to side to work the kinks out of her neck.

An evening discussing the Bible with Michael did sound good. But as long as she had to stay up baking all night and selling pies all day, it was a luxury she couldn't afford.

Michael's forehead puckered. "What would it take to put up a building here so you could bake at your convenience?"

Elizabeth stared. "I've been so focused on getting started, I haven't thought much further than just the moment at hand." She stepped out to the street and turned back to survey her property.

Could she do it? The thought of putting up her own building made her giddy.

"I wouldn't need to set out makeshift seating. I could make it large enough to have a dining area inside."

Michael stepped closer. "And a kitchen where you could bake while you're open for business. The smells will drive people wild."

"And a place to sleep," she said, envisioning her own quarters in the rear of the building. The benefits of the idea convinced her. She turned to Michael. "Would you be willing to escort me to the sawmill this afternoon? I need to get some prices."

❧

Elizabeth stared up at the rough wood building. Fresh paint glistened on the lettering over the door: CAPITAL RESTAURANT & BAKERY.

"What do you think?"

Michael beamed. "I like the name. It may not be the fanciest place in the town, but it serves the best pies around."

"I never thought I'd be able to keep working while this was going up, but we did it."

"*You* did it. This never would have happened without your grit and determination. And Prescott would have lost out on a fine new business."

Elizabeth smoothed her apron and smiled. "I can't believe I'll be able to work during the day and sleep all night. What luxury!"

"For awhile, maybe." Michael studied her, his eyes shadowed by concern. "When business picks up, you'll be just as busy as before. You need to hire someone, Elizabeth. You're strong, but you can't do it all on your own."

"I might, but I need to be sure I'm making enough to pay for the building before I take on another expense."

"If you don't spend a little more to give yourself some rest, you'll wind up losing the business anyway."

"I'll have you know I slept for five hours straight last night. I felt positively slothful." She chuckled at Michael's worried expression, then sobered. "All right, I'll consider hiring someone.

I know I can't keep up this pace much longer."

The relief in his eyes warmed her more than the morning sun. *Thank You, Lord, for sending me a friend like Michael, someone who accepts me as I am and likes me that way. Being able to talk to him is almost as good as having James around.*

No, better. The thought shook her to the soles of her shoes. She had left James behind in Philadelphia without a second thought, sure of his undying friendship but knowing they would keep in touch through the mail.

Could she do without Michael's presence so easily? Elizabeth tried to imagine spending her days without a glimpse of his dark, curly hair and ready smile. Without his stimulating conversation. Without his strength and support.

The thought painted a thoroughly dismal picture. And a frightening one.

When had she started relying on someone other than herself? If she intended to make her way on her own, could she afford this strong attachment she felt for him? Was it too late to back away?

And did she want to?

"I need to check on my pies. It wouldn't do to let them burn while I'm getting used to the new oven."

Michael followed her through the dining room and into the kitchen. He leaned on the counter and scooped up a glob of leftover dough with one finger.

"You never did tell me why you decided to start a bakery instead of selling mining supplies." He popped the dough into his mouth and smacked his lips.

Elizabeth opened the oven door and peeked at the pies inside. They still needed a few more minutes. "I needed something I could open right away and operate on a shoestring." Prompted by Michael's puzzled look, she recounted the way Richard had squandered her money.

"That's outrageous! The man ought to be horsewhipped."

"I would have been glad to volunteer, but it wouldn't have

gotten my money back." Michael's outrage cut through her assumed nonchalance. It felt good to have someone care. What would he say if she told him about the Bartletts' purpose in bringing her out to the territory? No, she could never do that. Even now, the memory made her blush. She could only imagine Michael's reaction. He'd probably offer to string Richard up from the nearest cottonwood.

And when did you start relying on a man to fight your battles for you, Elizabeth Simmons?

"I'm thinking about adding more to my menu. Serving full meals instead of just baked goods and coffee."

"Sounds good, if you can find the time. I still say you need to hire some help." He used another blob of dough to scrape a large drop of filling from the bottom of a bowl. "Mmm." He closed his eyes blissfully. "Do you cook as well as you bake?"

Elizabeth slid the pies from the oven to the counter. "That's just it. I don't. Soup is about the extent of my abilities. But I ought to be able to put together something simple, don't you think? Venison stew and biscuits, perhaps?"

"Sure, that's about all they serve over at the Juniper House, and I know I'd rather look at you while I'm eating than stare at Mr. Bernard's scruffy beard."

❧

Michael walked across the open plaza, enjoying the late afternoon sun. With this contract to deliver freight for the new mercantile, he was set for a profitable summer. Now, if he could keep his drivers on the road and the Indians from stealing his teams, he could begin to expand.

Glancing toward Elizabeth's bakery, he thought of heading over there to sample one of the new pastries she had added. No, better not. If he kept on eating her wares, more than his business would expand.

The tinny sounds of a saloon piano jarred his thoughts and filled the air with a crude melody. Knots of well-dressed men and women clustered along the west side of the plaza, looking across toward Whiskey Row. Michael shook his head. He would never cease to be amazed by the way Prescott's upstanding citizens felt comfortable standing and listening to the songs that emanated from the saloons, places they would never be seen entering.

The rapt expressions on the faces of a group opposite the Nugget caught his attention. Drawn by the haunting voice that floated across the way, he walked over to join them.

"Beautiful, isn't it?" the woman nearest him murmured.

Michael nodded, so captivated by the sweet tones he couldn't bring himself to speak. The clear notes drifted outside on the early summer breeze. The same voice singing the same song that had captured his interest once before.

"Each time I see the sun set
Beyond the distant hills,
My heart remembers how far you have gone.
So think of me each evening,
And until you come again,
I'll dream of you in our dear mountain home."

The song ended to raucous cheers from the saloon's patrons. The listeners on the plaza let out a collective sigh.

"What a lovely voice!" a woman exclaimed.

"Yes, it's a shame she chose to waste it in a barroom." Her male companion led her away, and the rest of the group dispersed.

Michael bristled at the comments. Did they really believe any woman would go into that life if she had any choice? And one with as sweet and pure a voice as that?

He turned to go back to his office, but his feet refused to carry him there. He looked back over his shoulder at the saloon. Someone rattled the piano keys in a noisy rendition of a Stephen Foster melody. Apparently, the singer was taking a break.

Michael started to leave again and, once more, found he couldn't. *What is it, Lord? Are You trying to tell me something?*

The Nugget pulled at him like a magnet, drawing him across the street. Michael followed the compulsion, wondering with every step what he was getting himself into.

When he reached the boardwalk, the jangling piano tune ceased, and the plaintive soprano voice started in again.

> "Brennan came riding across the broad moor,
> His beautiful maiden to find.
> 'Oh, where have they hidden that comely young lass,
> That raven-haired sweetheart of mine?' "

Michael reached the entrance of the Nugget. He gripped the top of the rough swinging door, clenching his hand until he could feel slivers of wood dig into his palm. *Lord, if this is You, You're leading me into some awfully strange places.*

Hoping he hadn't lost his mind, he pushed open the door and stepped into the saloon.

Michael blinked, adjusting his eyes to the dimness after the bright sunlight outside. No one paid the slightest attention to his entrance, which suited him fine. The saloons of Prescott were hardly his usual haunts, although his father spent plenty of time in them.

He sidled along the back wall to a pocket of shadow and stood riveted, his gaze focused on the girl on the stage.

The noisy hubbub ceased, and the men turned their attention to the singer, to all appearances as entranced as Michael.

The girl sang on, her eyes fixed on a point high above Michael's head, paying no heed to her audience. The lamplight created a halo effect around her blond hair and brought out its reddish glints. She was small, Michael noted, though taller than Elizabeth. Her frame seemed much too small to house such a glorious voice.

Lord, this is no hardened saloon girl. Look at that sweet face.

What is she doing here? Michael watched, fascinated by the contrast between her and the painted women hanging on the customers near the bar.

She wore a plain, pale blue dress and no makeup, hardly the garb one would expect in such a place. The dim lighting of the shadowy interior accentuated the deep wells of sadness in her eyes. The more he watched, the more Michael's confusion grew. Who could this girl be? And what was the purpose of his coming here?

The wistful song ended, and once again, the listening men offered loud applause. The young girl stepped off the low stage and made her way through the boisterous crowd, ignoring the crude comments and invitations as she shouldered past the leering patrons.

She started for the staircase at the back of the saloon. A burly, flat-eyed man near the bar shook his head and gestured toward the tables up front. The girl's face pinched in a look of pain.

Holding her head high despite her defeated expression, she walked toward a table where a rowdy group of miners greeted her with loose-lipped smiles.

"Come for a little visit, Darlin'? Here, you sweet thing, sit right down beside me."

"There's no room for another chair," another said. "She can sit on my lap." Bawdy laughter erupted as the speaker grabbed the girl's arm and pulled her toward him.

She shook free of his grip and edged away from the group. The man at the bar scowled and started toward her.

Without a second thought, Michael stepped forward and took the girl by the arm. She flinched and whirled to face him, wide-eyed.

He made an effort to control his anger and keep his voice even. "Would you join me over there?" He pointed to an empty table some distance from the pawing drunks.

She stared up at him like a frightened animal, jerking her

head back and forth as she looked first at him, then the man by the bar, then at Michael again. He could feel her tremble beneath his touch.

"I only want to talk to you."

Something in his tone seemed to steady her. She nodded briefly and sat down in the chair he held out for her. Michael saw the heavy man at the bar nod smugly.

"My name is Michael O'Roarke." He stared into eyes the color of turquoise. "Do you mind telling me who you are?"

After a long pause, she lowered her gaze to the table and answered. "I'm Jenny. Jenny Davis. And you're the first man who's spoken decently to me since I came here." She raised her head and studied him. "I don't remember seeing you before."

"I'm not exactly a regular. And if you'll forgive me for saying so, you don't look like you belong here, yourself."

Jenny's chin quivered. "I don't, Mister. I don't belong here at all."

"Then why. . . ?" Michael held up his hands, then dropped them on the table. "I shouldn't have asked. I'm sorry."

"No, it's all right. It just seems like a long time since anyone cared."

"Do you want to tell me about it?"

She hesitated, then nodded. "I've only been here a month or so. Up until then, I lived with my family on our farm out toward Chino Valley."

"Your family lives nearby, and they don't mind you being part of this?"

"That's just it. They aren't here anymore. They aren't anywhere." Her features grew taut, and she clenched her hands. "The Apaches raided our place a couple of months ago. They killed my ma and pa and my little brother, too. I was out in the root cellar the whole time, so they never knew I was there." She pressed the heels of her hands against her eyes. "But I saw the whole thing. And I heard it." A shudder ran through her body.

Michael reached out and laid his hand on her arm. This time she didn't flinch. "And you came here because you had nowhere else to go?"

She shook her head violently. "I would have died before I came to a place like this on my own. Martin Lester—he was a friend of my pa's—came by the day of the funeral. He showed me some papers where Pa had made him guardian for us kids if anything happened to our folks. Only I was the only one left." She squeezed her eyelids shut. Tiny crystal droplets appeared on her lashes.

"He took me home with him, said he was going to be a father to me. But he. . .he wanted to act more like a husband than a father."

Michael squeezed her hand. "You mean he forced himself on you?"

"No!" Jenny looked around nervously and lowered her voice. "He tried, but I fended him off time after time until he got tired of it. He said he'd spent plenty of money on my room and board and had to get some kind of return on it. So he brought me here. He knows the owner real well." She nodded toward the man at the bar. "That's Burleigh Ames. They're good friends. Martin traded me to Burleigh for a supply of whiskey."

"Traded you?" This time Michael was the one who had to lower his voice. "You mean he thinks he owns you?"

"He doesn't think so, Mister. He knows so."

"What does he have you do here?" Michael asked slowly, not sure he wanted to know the answer.

"He makes me sing for my room and board. So far, I've kept from having to go further, but he's pushing me in that direction all the time."

She laid her fingers on Michael's forearm, her touch as light as a butterfly's wing. "And it's wearing me down. I'm terrified I'll turn out to be like one of them." She flicked a glance toward the rear of the building, where two laughing women helped a drunken miner stagger up the back stairs.

She turned back to Michael and shook her head. "I don't know why I'm telling you this. Maybe it's because you're the first person who's been willing to listen."

"I think I know why." He'd been led here for a purpose; he felt sure of it. "How about if I help you get away from here?"

"You mean escape? Are you crazy? He'd kill me if I tried that."

"Where do you sleep?" At Jenny's startled look, Michael held up his hand. "I only need to know so I can plan the best way to get you out of here. What time do things settle down around here?"

"Everyone's pretty well gone by midnight. And my room's upstairs, right at the back."

"Can you stay awake until then? Be ready to meet me in the back alley at, say, one o'clock?"

Jenny's eyes were blue-green pools of wonder. "I can do that. But I still think you're crazy. Where am I supposed to go?"

Where indeed? He hadn't considered anything beyond actually getting Jenny off the premises. She would need a place to stay, someone strong to protect and guide her. A broad grin stretched across his face.

"I know just the place. You'll be safe there, I promise."

Jenny gave him a long, measuring look. He could understand her hesitation. After what she'd been through, why should she trust him. . .or any man, for that matter?

Finally, she nodded. "I don't know a thing about you, Michael O'Roarke, except your name and that you're a good listener. Whatever you have in mind, it can't be worse than what I've already gone through. I may be as crazy as you are, but I'll trust you."

"Good. I'll meet you out back, then. One o'clock."

Michael shouldered his way through the crowd. He caught Burleigh Ames glaring at him when he neared the door. *No, I didn't buy a drink, did I? And I'm going to cost you a lot more than that if my plan works out.*

fourteen

A heavy blanket of clouds massed overhead, shrouding the town and blocking out the moon's light. Michael crept along the alleyway behind the row of saloons.

His foot sent an empty bottle rattling across the gravel and he froze, listening. The darkness worked to his advantage in keeping him unseen, but he would have given a lot for just a bit of light right now.

A soft breeze stirred the treetops. From farther down the street, he heard a woman's shrill laugh. No one seemed to be aware of his presence, or if they were, they didn't care. He advanced a few yards farther and checked his position. The Nugget should be the next building down.

He picked his way along the alley and pressed against the wall. Now what? He should have arranged some sort of signal, but the thought hadn't occurred to him. Was Jenny still in her room or outside waiting for him?

He didn't want to risk making a sound, but he didn't have much choice. "Jenny?" The low whisper wasn't much louder than the breeze.

A dark figure detached itself from the blackness and moved toward him. "I'm here."

She wore a hooded cloak of a dark material that blended into the night. When she raised her head, he could just make out the pale oval of her face.

Michael put his arm around her shoulders and felt her muscles tense. "Don't be afraid. I just need to know where you are so I can guide us out of here."

They moved through the darkness step by cautious step. Michael's pulse raced in direct contrast to their slow pace.

Every instinct screamed at him to run, but to do so would be to invite discovery.

The hair on the back of his neck stood on end. At any moment, he expected the rear door of the Nugget to fly open to reveal Burleigh Ames in pursuit.

They reached Gurley Street without incident, and Michael allowed himself to believe they might actually make good their escape.

"Do you know where we are?"

Jenny shook her head. "I hardly ever came into town when we lived on the farm. And I haven't been outside once since Burleigh had me."

"We're going to follow this street for a ways, then cross the plaza. Come on." He took her hand and led the way.

Near the middle of the plaza, Jenny pulled back. "Where are you taking me?"

"To the Capital Bakery, just ahead. It belongs to a friend of mine. A woman friend." Jenny hesitated only a moment, then allowed him to guide her the rest of the way.

At Elizabeth's back door, she gripped his arm. "She didn't mind the idea of taking me in, once she knew where I've been?"

I knew I forgot something. "I'm sure she'll be happy to help." Michael raised his hand and tapped on the door.

"You mean you haven't told her about me?" Jenny's voice rose in panic. "She doesn't know I'm coming?"

"Don't worry. It'll be fine." *Lord, please let it be all right.*

❧

Elizabeth stood outside her home in Philadelphia. All the lights were on, as though a party was in progress. She reached for the ornate knocker and let it fall.

Tap. Tap. Tap.

Why didn't they let her in? Why didn't someone answer the door?

Tap. Tap.

Elizabeth rolled over and sat up in her bed. Her hair

draped over her shoulder in a loose braid. She wiped the sleep from her eyes, amazed at how real her dream had seemed.

Tap. Tap.

The low murmur of voices carried into her sleeping quarters. Elizabeth scrubbed her face with her hands and got up, pulling a blanket around her shoulders.

Padding across the plank floor in her bare feet, she pressed her lips close to the back door. "Who is it?"

"It's Michael. I need your help."

She glanced down at her thin nightgown. She really ought to go get dressed first, but he sounded desperate. She wrapped the blanket more closely around her and swung the door open.

"Michael, what time is it? What. . . ?" She scrabbled for a match.

"Don't light the lamp until the door's closed. We need to get inside without being seen."

We? For the first time she noticed the dark figure behind him. The strain in his voice told her something was seriously wrong. "Come inside, then. Hurry." She bolted the door and lit the lamp.

Michael, dressed in dark pants and shirt, looked at her with an anxious gaze and turned his hat in his hands. Beside him stood a wary-eyed young girl in a deep blue cloak.

Elizabeth glanced down at her nightgown, bare toes, and makeshift wrap, then back at Michael. "Would you mind telling me what's going on?"

"This is Jenny Davis." Michael urged the girl forward. "She needs a place to stay."

You bring a total stranger—and a lovely one at that—to my door in the dead of night and expect me to make her welcome? What is going on, Michael O'Roarke?

The silence grew while he hesitated. Jenny stared at Elizabeth as if expecting her to order her back outside. Her chin lifted defiantly, a gesture that reminded Elizabeth of herself.

"You don't have to let me stay if you don't want to," she said. "I'll understand."

Elizabeth's gaze met Michael's over the girl's head. He sent her a pleading glance and silently mouthed, "Please."

Whatever was happening here, it was plain Michael needed her help. "Of course you may stay," she said.

Michael's shoulders sagged in obvious relief, and he gave the girl's shoulder a squeeze. "You're in good hands for tonight, Jenny. I'll come back in the morning, and we'll figure out what to do next."

"You're leaving?" Jenny's tone bordered on panic.

"Just for a few hours. You'll be safe here, I promise."

"He can stay a few minutes longer while I fix a place for you to sleep." Elizabeth gave Michael a look that dared him to do otherwise. She hurried to the storeroom, where she piled folded blankets on the floor to make a pallet. Another blanket, rolled tight and stuffed into a pillowcase, would serve as a pillow. Not fancy lodgings, by any means, but adequate for one night. Or what was left of it.

She returned to find Michael watching Jenny, who sagged in a chair. "Your room is just around the corner," Elizabeth told her. "You might as well get settled in for the night." Jenny took the candle Elizabeth handed her and left without a word.

Michael opened the door and stepped outside. "I'll see you in the morning."

"Not so fast." Elizabeth followed him and closed the door behind her. "I'll never get a wink of sleep until I have some answers. Who is your friend, and why is she here?"

"I don't know much about her. I just met her today."

Elizabeth folded her arms. "You certainly build up acquaintances quickly." She felt great satisfaction when he squirmed under her scrutiny.

"I heard her singing at the Nugget—"

"Wait a minute. You're leaving a saloon girl on my doorstep?"

"So I went inside—"

"Now you frequent saloons?"

"And she told me her story."

"I'll bet it was a good one."

"It'll melt your heart." Michael gave a quick overview of Jenny's situation. "She needs a place to stay and someone to protect her. I'll admit I should have asked you first—"

"I won't argue with that."

"But you were the only person I could think of. I couldn't very well take her home with me, could I?"

Not and live to tell about it. "You're right. She needs a place to stay, and I'll keep her for the night. But I'd better not find some gun-toting saloon keeper banging on my door in the middle of the night."

Michael's grin lit up in the moonlight. "Heaven help him if he does."

Elizabeth bolted the door and pushed a chair in front of it for good measure, then carried the lamp to the storeroom. "Do you have everything you need?"

Jenny perched on a sack of flour, still wrapped in her hooded cloak. With her arms folded tightly across her chest and the sullen expression she wore, she reminded Elizabeth of a sulky twelve year old.

"You don't want me here, do you?" The bald statement caught Elizabeth off guard.

"You took me by surprise, that's all. I'm not in the habit of having callers in the wee hours. Do you need to borrow a nightgown?"

"I'll sleep in my dress. I don't want to put you out any more than I already have. Don't worry, I'll be out of your way tomorrow." She loosened the tie at her throat and let the cloak slide off her shoulders.

It took all the restraint Elizabeth could muster to keep from reaching out to touch the golden hair. Gold, with hints of burnished copper, just like Carrie's. "You have beautiful hair," she managed to say.

Jenny looked directly at her for the first time. Blue-green eyes. Carrie's eyes. Elizabeth felt swept away on a wave of homesickness. She remembered the story Michael had whispered to her on the doorstep. "How old are you?"

Jenny's chin jutted forward. "Eighteen."

Only two years older than Carrie. An image of her sister, bereft of family and forced into an intolerable situation, crossed Elizabeth's mind, melting away her suspicion and doubt.

"Jenny, you're welcome here. You can stay with me as long as you like."

Elizabeth lay awake long after she blew out the lamp. She wanted to help Jenny, but. . .how did Michael just happen to come across her, and exactly what did Jenny mean to him?

She's lovely; there's no denying it.

She sighed and punched the pillow, longing for sleep that wouldn't come.

❧

"Is there something I can do to help?"

Elizabeth turned from the counter. Jenny stood diffidently in the doorway, a shy expression replacing the sullen stare of the night before.

"I'm surprised you're up so early. Did you sleep at all?" The dark circles under Jenny's eyes gave her the answer.

Jenny moved two steps closer and peered into the pot Elizabeth was stirring. "What are you doing?"

"Trying to salvage what's left of these mashed potatoes. I'd planned to offer them as part of today's lunch, but they're too runny."

"You ruined mashed potatoes? How could you do that?"

"I managed." Elizabeth wiped her forehead with her sleeve. "I'm afraid cooking is not my strong point."

Jenny moved right up next to her. "It looks like you forgot to drain them."

"You drain them first?" Elizabeth stared at the pot. "Is there any way to fix them?"

Jenny offered her a smile. "You can chop some onion into it and call it potato soup."

Elizabeth laughed ruefully. "So you know how to cook?"

"My ma taught me. I've been doing it for years."

"And you enjoy it?"

"Sure, doesn't everyone?" She grinned. "I don't bake very well, but I can fix a pot roast that'll make your mouth water."

Elizabeth tapped her fingers on the counter. "How would you like a job?"

"Where? You mean here? With you?"

"If you're willing to fix the main meals and teach me to cook, I'll pay you plus give you room and board. What do you think?"

"You'll pay me just to cook?"

"For a large crowd of very hungry men."

"And I can stay here?"

"We'll fix up a more suitable place for you this evening. What do you think, Jenny? You'll be safe here. I won't let anybody hurt you. Do we have a deal?"

Jenny's turquoise eyes misted. "When do I start?"

"Right now. Go out front and add potato soup to the menu."

fifteen

You've done wonders with Jenny." Michael cupped his hand under Elizabeth's elbow when she stepped down off the boardwalk.

"She's done wonders for me, you mean. I can't believe I actually have time to stroll outdoors like this. I'm not hurrying out for supplies, just taking a little time to relax. Jenny's doing a wonderful job of handling things, although I only leave her on her own when I know she won't have to deal with a crowd of customers." They walked across Cortez Street and circled the perimeter of the plaza. A dusty haze softened the glare of the westering sun and gave the scene a gentle glow.

Elizabeth sauntered alongside Michael, content just to enjoy the pleasure of his company. When they turned back in the direction of the restaurant, she felt her steps dragging. It would be nice to shake off responsibility for just one day, to leave the demands of her business behind and go for a picnic under the pines with Michael.

Across the street, a figure strode toward them. Elizabeth stiffened when she recognized Letitia Bartlett. Letitia noticed Elizabeth at the same moment. She stood stock-still and stared directly at her. Even at that distance, Elizabeth could see the malevolent gleam in her eyes. Letitia's lips curled back in a snarl. She stretched her arm out like a prophetess pronouncing judgment and pointed straight at Elizabeth, her thin hand trembling wildly.

Suddenly, the restaurant seemed like the perfect place to be. Before she could say a word, Michael took her arm and veered between two buildings, safely out of the reach of Letitia Bartlett.

Elizabeth cast one last glance over her shoulder. Letitia stood in the same position, like a statue, still staring, still pointing.

"Thank you," she said, hurrying to keep pace with Michael's long strides.

He patted her hand where she clutched at his elbow. "I had a feeling she was the last person in the world you wanted to see right now."

"I'm ashamed to admit it, but you're right." She hadn't seen Letitia since that explosive morning in the Bartletts' kitchen and didn't care to renew her acquaintance. Her breath came in quick gasps. "I think we can slow down now."

"Sure, we're almost there anyway." He reached for the knob to open the door.

Elizabeth entered eagerly. Never before had it seemed such a place of refuge. She looked around the empty dining room with a sense of coming home.

Home. Despite her near miss with Letitia, excitement rippled inside her. She walked to the window and planted her hands on the sill.

Outside, the laughter of early evening strollers gave an air of peace to this place. It was a good place.

Her place.

Elizabeth's heart swelled. Out here in this raw land, she had found the focus for her life, the place where she could truly be herself. This restaurant would be a place of shelter, a haven for both herself and Jenny.

"Thank you for that wonderful break, Michael. It was just what I needed." She turned back to him, stood on her toes, and kissed his cheek. "Good night."

❧

"Where is she?" The rasping voice carried all the way back to the kitchen.

Jenny hurried in from the dining room, round-eyed. "Someone's asking for you."

"So I heard." Elizabeth covered a mound of pie crust

dough with a damp dish towel and wiped the flour from her hands before going to see who the belligerent visitor might be. She pushed open the swinging door and stopped as though she'd walked into a tree.

The walls of her sanctuary had been breached.

Letitia Bartlett stood in the center of the dining room, her mouth set in a grim line, body rigid, face contorted. "So here you are!"

Not here, not in front of her customers. "Let's go into the back, shall we?" Elizabeth gripped the woman's bony arm and propelled her past Jenny and the gaping patrons.

Letitia shook off Elizabeth's hand as soon as they reached the kitchen. "Was this your plan all along?"

Elizabeth looked around at the restaurant she had built. "My plan?" She edged away, wishing she hadn't positioned Letitia between her and the door. The woman's manner seemed positively demented.

"Don't play the innocent with me!" An ugly red color suffused Letitia's face. She moved closer to Elizabeth. "You played us for fools from the beginning, didn't you?"

What could she use to defend herself? Elizabeth took a quick inventory of the items within her reach: spoons, bowls, a pastry cloth—those wouldn't be of any use. The maple rolling pin might come in handy, though.

She tried to inject a soothing note into her voice. "I'm not sure what you mean."

Letitia swept her arm along the counter, knocking three freshly baked pies to the floor. "Did you imagine we wouldn't find out?"

Lord, help me! She's gone crazy.

Letitia continued to advance. Elizabeth took a step back and bumped against the counter. Without taking her gaze off Letitia, she stretched out her hand along the wooden surface. Her fingers closed around the rolling pin and gripped it tight.

"I saw you yesterday. Don't try to deny it. I know you saw me too, even though you tried to pretend you didn't."

Was that what this tirade was all about?

"How long have the two of you been walking out together?"

Elizabeth shook her head slowly. "What does this have to do with Michael?"

"Which one of you came up with the idea to cheat us out of our money, you or him?"

"Cheat you? Whatever are you talking about?"

"As if you didn't know! I'm talking about the money we were promised for bringing you together."

Elizabeth pressed her free hand against her throbbing temple. "Does this have something to do with your arrangement to sell me off as someone's wife?" The memory of that nightmare made her temper flare anew.

"Spare me your theatrics. I'll admit you had us fooled, standing there in our kitchen and acting so horrified at the idea of us making you a fine match. And here you've been seeing him behind our backs all the time!"

Letitia's accusation sliced through the confusing fog like a lighthouse beacon. From the dining room, Elizabeth could hear low voices and the faint clink of silverware. Out there, life went on as usual. In the kitchen, time stood still.

She let go of the rolling pin and clasped her hands against her middle. When she was five, a visiting relative's son had punched her in the stomach. She felt the same sense of shock, the same inability to breathe now.

Only back then, James had been around to come to her aid, giving the boy a taste of his own medicine before sending him howling back to his parents.

James wasn't here now.

Michael was.

Michael.

Closing her eyes against the pain, she focused all her efforts on drawing one long, deep breath. "Are you saying that

Michael O'Roarke is the man you were supposed to find a wife for?"

"He's Timothy O'Roarke's son, isn't he?"

Elizabeth wrapped one arm around her roiling stomach and used the other to pull herself up.

"Get out." She lifted her head and stared straight at Letitia.

"Don't think you've heard the last of this."

"I said, get out of my restaurant. Now."

Letitia started to speak, then took another look at Elizabeth's face. She snapped her mouth closed and left without another word.

Elizabeth let herself sink down to the floor. The hard surface bit into her knees but couldn't hold a candle to the pain that twisted through her heart.

Michael, a party to the Bartletts' sordid scheme?

She couldn't believe it—didn't want to believe it.

But Letitia's anger had been all too real.

She wrapped both arms around her middle and rocked forward until her head rested on her knees. Hadn't Michael supported her, encouraged her, shown her friendship? But he'd never mentioned his father, not once. Because he and his father didn't get along or because he didn't want to admit to being in on a devious plot?

She remembered his outrage on learning how Richard had squandered her money. Had his indignation been real or feigned?

Just yesterday, he had seemed to pick up on her unwillingness to face Letitia and helped her hurry away. A chivalrous gesture or an attempt to keep her from learning the truth?

Her Michael, a deceiver?

And when, she wondered, had she started thinking of him as "her" Michael?

No more. She wiped her tear-soaked cheeks with her palms and pulled herself to her feet. She would have to deal with Michael's perfidy another time.

Right now, there were customers to attend to and pies to bake.

ও

"Are you all right?" Jenny asked, coming into the kitchen.

Elizabeth slapped a ball of pie crust dough onto the counter. "Why do you ask?"

Jenny watched her pound it into a flat, round disk with the side of her fist. "Didn't you tell me light pastry required a light touch? You look like you'd rather be punching someone in the face."

The idea didn't sound half bad. At the moment, she had no lack of ideas for potential targets. Still, her customers didn't need to suffer for her inner turmoil. She stepped back from the counter and took a series of slow, calming breaths.

"It was that woman, wasn't it?" Jenny went on. "The one who came in here this morning. You've barely spoken since she left."

Elizabeth rolled the dough out with smooth, even strokes and settled the crust into a waiting pie tin. "She said some things that upset me, but I shouldn't be taking it out on you. You had nothing to do with it." *Unless Michael O'Roarke planned to deceive you, too. In which case, I will most definitely punch him in the nose!*

Jenny brightened. "I'm glad. I was afraid I might have done something wrong."

"No, I just found out I was wrong about someone, and that's never pleasant. But I'll get over it. No harm's been done." *Except to my pride. And my heart.*

She rolled out the rest of the dough and lined the other pie tins. Cutting vents into the top crusts for the steam to escape and crimping the edges together kept her hands in motion, soothing her with the practiced motions of a familiar task. She slid the four pies into the oven.

"There. While those are baking, how about that lesson in making gravy?"

❧

Jenny dipped a spoon into the gravy and brought it to her lips. "Perfect," she proclaimed.

"It can't be," Elizabeth stated. "I've never made perfect gravy in my life or any that was remotely close to perfect." She sampled her own spoonful, and her eyes widened. "It isn't bad, is it? I can't believe it. Why didn't anyone ever tell me cooking could be this much fun?"

"Wait until I teach you to make fried chicken. Then we'll try baked ham."

"And roast turkey?"

"That, too." A knock at the back door interrupted their laughter.

"I'll get it." Jenny pulled off her apron and started toward the door.

"No, let me." Elizabeth hurried past her. The thought that Burleigh Ames could be searching for Jenny kept Elizabeth vigilant.

She pulled the door open a crack and looked out.

"It's a beautiful evening," Michael said, smiling. "How about a walk in the moonlight?"

Angry tears stung her eyes, and she blinked them back. She would not show him how he'd hurt her.

"I can't, Michael, I'm much too busy tonight."

His smile dimmed only a fraction. "Then why don't I come in, and we can talk while you work?"

"No, Jenny and I have a lot to do. Girl things." She started to close the door. Michael reached up and blocked it with his palm. Concern creased his forehead.

"Tomorrow, then? I can come by right after you close."

Elizabeth felt her throat closing. A deep heartache compressed her chest. "I'm afraid I'm going to be unavailable then, too. It's a really busy time." Michael stared at her a moment, then withdrew his hand and walked away.

She bolted the door before he could say anything more.

Tears threatened, and she turned to hurry to her room before they spilled over. Jenny stood behind her, leaning against the wall with her arms folded.

"It's him, isn't it? I thought it was just that awful old woman, but it has something to do with Michael, too, doesn't it?"

Elizabeth held her head high and tried to draw a deep breath. Instead, she heard a ragged gasp. She squeezed her eyelids shut. She would not cry. She would not lose control.

The tears slid past her closed lids and down her cheeks. She felt Jenny's arm slip around her shoulders.

"Even a white knight gets knocked off his horse sometimes. Now, what are those girl things we're going to be doing this evening?"

sixteen

Elizabeth stood by the counter watching Jenny work, but her thoughts kept going back over the last week. She truly had kept busy, but mostly to prevent herself from thinking too much.

"Like this?" Jenny lapped one side of the thin circle of dough over the other and lifted it cautiously. The tip of her tongue protruded from one corner of her mouth.

"That's right." Elizabeth fought back the urge to reach out and help. Jenny had to learn on her own—was determined to, in fact. Elizabeth had come to realize that Jenny had a streak of independence that rivaled her own.

Jenny settled the folded dough in place atop a peach pie, then spread it open again and let out a pent-up breath. "I always have a problem with the next part." She pressed the tip of her thumb and the knuckle of her first finger at the rim of the pie plate, then used her other thumb to push the overlapping dough into the vee they formed.

She looked at her work and beamed. "That looks pretty good, though, doesn't it?"

"Just right," Elizabeth affirmed.

Jenny continued to work around the rim of the pie, methodically crimping the edges. Elizabeth dampened a cloth and began wiping down the counter.

"You're getting better every day, Jenny. Pretty soon, I'll be able to turn all the cooking over to you."

Jenny laughed. "Not anytime soon. I still don't quite have the hang of this." Her hands moved in rhythm now, pinching and pushing the dough into sharp peaks.

"You'll see." Elizabeth scooped the loose flour into a pile and swept it off the counter into her cupped hand. "Before long, I'll be able to sit back and become a lady of leisure. I thank God every day that He brought you here. But I'm sure you've already thanked Him plenty of times for getting you out of the hands of men like your guardian and that saloon keeper."

Jenny's hands stilled. Elizabeth could see the girl's shoulders tense beneath her light blue dress. "No, and that won't happen anytime soon, either," Jenny murmured. She shoved the dough into a lopsided mound. "I don't think God is all that interested in hearing what I have to say."

Elizabeth paused in the act of dusting the flour off her hands. "You aren't serious, are you? Of course He is. God loves you, Jenny."

"Really? He sure has a funny way of showing it." Her hands moved like uncoordinated pistons.

"He brought you here. He got you out of that horrid place."

"I wound up there because I wouldn't put up with Martin Lester's advances. And that wouldn't have happened if my parents hadn't died." Jenny's voice choked off.

"But surely you can see—"

"Do you have any idea what it's like to hide in the darkness of a root cellar and know your family's being massacred? To hear your ma plead for mercy and find none?"

"Jenny, I—"

"To peek out long enough to see your little brother run away and try to get back to the cabin, then hear him scream and know he didn't make it?" She picked up a lump of dough and squeezed it until it oozed through her fingers.

Elizabeth kneaded the damp cloth in her hands, praying for the right words. But how could any words make sense of Jenny's loss? "I can't answer that. I have no idea why He would allow that to happen. All I can say is that He must have something planned for you, some reason you were spared."

"Spared?" Jenny slammed her hand on the counter, flattening the dough under her palm. "You call it being spared when I live with those images every day of my life? When I wake up at night thinking I hear my mama screaming?"

"But the Bible says—"

"I know. I remember the stories. He's supposed to love everyone. I thought He loved me. Maybe He did, once. But He didn't love me when that was happening. And He can't love me anymore. Not after the saloon."

"That wasn't your doing, any of it. You didn't choose to be in that place."

Jenny picked up the dough again and rolled it into a ball. "Being pawed like that was enough to make me feel like I'd already become like those other girls. But I never did go upstairs with any man. Not once. And it wasn't all the men who came in there who were bad. Some of them just ignored me. It was the other ones, the ones who'd had too much to drink. They'd grab me when I walked by, grab me and. . ." She threw down the dough and covered her face with her hands. Her shoulders heaved.

Elizabeth wrapped her arms around the sobbing girl and pulled her close. "It's over, Jenny. Over for good. No one is going to treat you like that again." She stroked the soft golden hair. "And Jenny? You can trust God. He does love you."

Jenny straightened and backed away, mopping her blotchy face with her hands. "What about Michael? I think he loves you, but you don't trust him." She turned on her heel and ran to her room.

Elizabeth stared after her. "Oh, Lord, how do I get through to her? It's not the same at all. Michael couldn't love me and be a party to that vile scheme. I don't *want* him to love me. Do I?"

❧

Michael's horse brought him through the trees to the edge of town. His mule herd was grazing about three miles from Fort Whipple, and the herders hadn't had any trouble from Indians. His competition had all lost animals to raids, but so far, God continued to protect his business.

His stomach growled on the way down the hill into town. He could go home and make do with whatever he could find on his shelves. *But I want a real meal.* He reached the plaza. The Pine Cone Eatery would have chili, if his stomach could handle all the chili powder they used to cover up the taste of spoiled meat.

He glanced across the plaza, and his gaze locked on the Capital Restaurant. The pain of being ignored warred with his longing for a good meal.

Hunger won out. As soon as he put his horse away, he'd wash off the trail dust and head straight for the restaurant and a decent supper.

If Elizabeth didn't throw him out.

Michael pondered the situation all the while he brushed and fed his horse and sluiced water over his head and arms. Elizabeth's first refusal to go walking had puzzled him, but he'd put it down to pressures of the business. That he could accept. But her subsequent rejections didn't seem to have any logical explanation. He put on a clean shirt and headed out the door. Maybe the extra hours spent training Jenny were taking their toll.

Jenny. Michael snapped his fingers. Could Jenny have done something to cause Elizabeth's sudden change in attitude?

But that didn't explain why she'd taken such a sudden aversion to him. Unless she blamed him for Jenny's presence in her life. Michael nodded his head. *It's my fault.*

Looking back, he knew he'd made a mistake in not telling Elizabeth about his plans to rescue Jenny ahead of time. He thought she'd taken their surprise midnight visit rather well, but obviously, that wasn't the case. That must be it. He grinned, pleased at having discovered the source of the trouble.

He crossed the plaza with a lighter step. A man couldn't fix a problem if he didn't know what was wrong. Now that he did, he would talk to Elizabeth, apologize, and get back in her good graces.

He could spend time at the restaurant again without feeling like a pariah. She'd even go out walking with him again. That would be nice. He really missed her company.

He missed her spunk, her wit. Missed her smile and that green fire in her eyes when she got riled.

"Face it," he told himself, "you miss *her*, pure and simple. This is more than friendship."

He felt the truth of his words. Without him noticing, Elizabeth had captured his heart. . .had become so much a part of the fabric of his life that he couldn't imagine having any kind of happiness without her.

With a prayer for God to work it all out, he walked into the restaurant. Jenny stood taking an order from a table of miners. He smiled and gave her a brief wave, then sat down near the window. When she came to take his order, he could ask to see Elizabeth.

He would offer his apology, she would accept, and things would smooth out just fine. Heartened by the knowledge that they'd soon be laughing over their little misunderstanding, he scanned the menu tacked to a board on the wall. His stomach rumbled as he perused the list: venison steak, roast beef, venison pie. . . . The roast beef, he decided. Just the thing for a hungry man who wanted something tasty under his belt before he had to dine on crow.

Jenny headed his way, a smile of welcome lighting her face as she threaded her way between the tables.

"Well, hello, little darlin'." A grimy, middle-aged man scooted his chair back, barring her way. Jenny halted abruptly, then gave him a tight smile and circled to her left.

The man stood quickly and blocked her path. "Don't you recognize me, sweet thing?"

Other customers interrupted their conversations and turned to watch. Jenny's eyes darted back and forth like a hunted animal seeking a way to escape.

A pulse throbbed in Michael's throat. He jumped to his

feet and waded through a sea of empty chairs, shoving them aside like Moses parting the waters.

"Aw, come on. I know you remember. When you were singing over at the Nugget, I used to think your songs were meant just for me." The man made a lunge for Jenny's wrist. Michael redoubled his speed.

Before he could reach Jenny, the door to the kitchen flew open and a whirlwind erupted.

"What do you think you're doing?" Elizabeth, all five foot two of her, glared up at the man, a diminutive David ready to take on Goliath.

"No need to get upset, little lady. I'm just renewing an old acquaintance. This little gal and I are friends from the Nugget, aren't we?" He gave Jenny a suggestive wink. She pivoted on her heel and escaped through the swinging door to the kitchen.

Elizabeth pointed to the door. "Get out of my restaurant before I have you arrested."

"This doesn't concern you." His meaty hand reached out as if to brush Elizabeth aside.

Michael blocked the movement by grabbing a handful of the man's shirt and swinging him around in one motion. "You heard the lady. It's time to leave."

Jenny's tormentor started to swing, then took a second look at Michael and reconsidered. He stepped back, loosening the wad of fabric at his throat.

"Sure, Mister. There's no problem here. Just a little misunderstanding, that's all." He picked up his hat and backed toward the door, giving Michael a wide berth.

Not until the door swung shut behind the retreating form did Michael turn back to Elizabeth. "Are you all right?"

She nodded, her eyes still focused on the doorway. "Thank you for stepping in." Her gaze met his for a brief moment, then skittered away. "Jenny needs me," she muttered and disappeared into the kitchen.

The other customers, deprived of any better entertainment, focused their attention on him. Michael looked once more at the list of delectable offerings, then headed for the front door and home.

His appetite had disappeared.

❧

"Jenny?" Elizabeth tapped again on the girl's door and huffed out a frustrated sigh when she got no answer. That Jenny needed to be with someone was obvious. That she had every intention of keeping the rest of the world—Elizabeth included—at arm's length was equally clear.

Elizabeth pressed her forehead against the door frame. She needed to see Jenny, talk to her, and make sure she was all right. Together, they could pray and lay the whole ugly incident in the hands of the only One who could take the pain out of Jenny's past.

She needed to get back to her customers, especially now that it appeared she would be waiting tables and manning the kitchen on her own for the time being. She needed to decide what to say to Michael back in the dining room.

I can't go that many directions at once, Lord! The wood bit into her forehead. She pushed away from the door frame and rubbed the tender spot, hoping the pressure hadn't left a mark. The last thing she needed right now was one more reason for her customers to gawk at her.

That odious man! The memory of his effrontery and Jenny's white face brought the moment back all over again. What right did he have, coming into her place of business and casting aspersions on Jenny's character, right in front of a roomful of people?

If Michael hadn't stepped in when he did. . .

If Michael hadn't stepped in, she'd have thrown the lout out herself. His willingness to help had been appreciated, though surprising, but she would have been perfectly capable of handling the situation on her own.

Just like she'd be capable of going on with the rest of her life without Michael's assistance. The knowledge left a raw wound, but she reminded herself of the need to be strong. How could she ever trust someone who would stoop to scheming with the Bartletts?

She couldn't. Life had seemed for a moment to hold such promise. But the lovely dream had turned out to be a nightmare instead. She would have to wake up to reality and go on.

Bracing herself for the encounter, she pushed through the door to the dining room. A dozen faces, still alive with curiosity, turned to greet her.

None of them belonged to Michael.

Her shoulders sagged, and she felt as though the wind had been let out of her sails. Relief, she assured herself.

Really? That empty sensation felt a lot like disappointment.

Disappointment? At not seeing Michael O'Roarke? Ridiculous! She had no patience with the man and not the slightest desire to talk to him again, not after what he had done.

seventeen

"Pssst!"

From his vantage point behind a bush across the alley behind the restaurant, Michael watched Jenny jump as if shot and fall back against the building's rough wooden exterior. Maybe he should have made his presence known a little more openly.

"It's me," he said, standing and stepping out into the alley behind the restaurant.

"Michael!" Jenny fanned herself with her hand and looked down at the old flour sack filled with loose garbage she'd dropped in her fright. Bones, peels, and egg shells lay strewn in the dust. "I thought it was—well, never mind." She stooped and started gathering the trash.

She thought it was Martin Lester, come to take her back, you idiot! "Let me do that." He knelt beside her and picked up a handful of garbage.

"Have at it." Jenny stood and left him to deal with the smelly mess. "I think you scared me out of a year's growth."

Remorse warred with his reason for lurking in the bushes like a thief. "I needed to talk to you."

"Most people would come inside the restaurant to do that."

"No, I need to talk to you. Just you, without Elizabeth around." He picked up the reeking mass of garbage and held it out in front of him. Whatever was dripping found its way down his arm and soaked into his sleeve.

"You won't be able to sneak up on anyone now." Jenny wrinkled her nose and took two steps away from him.

He dropped the sack into the barrel and wiped his hands off. The smell still lingered. He moved downwind from Jenny,

132

wishing he could move upwind of himself. "It's about Elizabeth," he began. "What's going on? I thought she enjoyed spending time with me, but now she won't give me the time of day."

Jenny's eyes grew round. "You mean you don't know?" She shook her head. "The way she's been acting, I was certain the two of you had some kind of argument."

"Nope. One day we're the best of friends, and the next she's refusing to walk out with me and treating me like a leper. I was hoping you'd know."

Jenny's brow furrowed. "She hasn't been the same since that horrid woman came to the restaurant. Something was said that upset Elizabeth, I'm sure of it, but I have no idea what it was. . .or what connection you have with it all."

"Connection? Me?" Michael's mind whirled as he tried—and failed—to make some sense of what he heard. What woman? What had she said? And how could it possibly involve him?

"I'd better get back inside." Jenny's voice interrupted his thoughts. "Elizabeth worries if I'm outside on my own. And for a moment there, I thought she was right!" She gave a shaky laugh.

Michael put out his hand to stop her. "If you hear anything about what I'm supposed to have done, will you let me know?" He gave Jenny a quick hug. "And I'm sorry I scared you."

Jenny's half smile spoke of her pity for his plight. "I'll do what I can to find out," she promised. "But don't get your hopes up too high."

"What if I wait out here every night and try to catch Elizabeth?"

"I'm the one who takes the trash out." Jenny smiled. "You might do better not to scare her like you did me."

❧

"Excuse me, we'd like to place our order." The plump matron waved Elizabeth toward her table in the manner of a queen summoning an underling.

Elizabeth shifted the tray of dirty dishes to one hip and tried to smile. "I'll let Jenny know you're ready," she told the woman and her two companions. "She'll be right out."

"Just a moment." The spokeswoman held up her hand in an imperious gesture, halting Elizabeth's escape. "We would prefer you did it. I have heard that the food is good here, but I have no desire to have any dealings with. . ." She lowered her voice. "She *is* the one who used to work at that awful saloon, is she not?" Her lower chin wobbled indignantly as her companions nodded their agreement.

Elizabeth set the tray down on a neighboring table with a crash, unmindful of the rattle of crockery. Her anger erupted in a rush. "Jenny Davis is a fine young woman, with more decency than the three of you put together!"

All three ladies squawked in protest. "How dare you speak to us like that!" their leader demanded. "We will not be treated this way!"

"Then maybe you would prefer eating elsewhere." Elizabeth fixed the trio with a gimlet stare while they gathered their things and trooped out. She swept up the tray and made her way back to the kitchen, ignoring the stares that followed her. Would this kind of thing keep happening? *How does a person restore a damaged reputation?*

At least Jenny hadn't heard the disparaging comments. . .this time. But what about the next time? And the next?

It would be so much easier for Jenny if she let God be a part of her life. Then she could let Him help her carry her burdens. And Jenny had plenty of those. *I don't know what to say to her. I don't know why You let all those things happen or why this is happening now. Maybe You can even use something like this to draw Jenny to You, although it's hard for me to see how.*

Despite her anger at her three former customers, she felt a small thrill of victory. She'd dealt with today's confrontation—without the help of Michael O'Roarke. The knowledge brought mingled pleasure and pain.

❧

"I'll take this trash out, Jenny."

Jenny scrambled for a dish towel and wiped her hands free of soapsuds. "I can do it. I don't mind."

"No, you go on washing those dishes. You've taken care of the trash every night for a week now. I'm surprised you haven't complained about having to handle the smelly stuff."

"You may be surprised about more than just that."

Elizabeth had to strain to hear Jenny's cryptic remark. With a quizzical glance, she gathered up the rubbish and went out. Outside, she savored a long, slow breath of the evening air. Look at that sunset! Thumb Butte wore its display of vivid violets and crimsons like a royal robe. It would be wonderful just to walk among the pines and enjoy all this beauty as she used to with Michael. Before. She dumped the lard tin into the garbage barrel and turned to go back inside.

Michael stood waiting on the doorstep.

Elizabeth eyed him warily. Arms folded across his chest, feet planted well apart, he looked like a man ready to withstand an army.

Shock surged into anger. The nerve of the man, thinking he could intimidate her by blocking the way to her own door! She could go right through him if she needed to.

She crossed her arms and prepared for battle. "What do you think you're doing here?"

"I've come for an explanation."

Elizabeth felt the heat rise from her neck to her hairline. She took one step forward, and Michael raised his hands, turning them palm out in a gesture of surrender.

"Please," he said.

The appeal brought her up short, and she looked at him more closely. The same curly, dark hair, the same vivid blue eyes. The same smile that always set her heart dancing. The same features that always made her think of him as her Michael.

How could her Michael look just as before yet cause her heart so much pain? Her Michael? Not anymore.

He seemed to take her hesitation as a sign of a truce and took an eager step forward. "It seems I've done something to upset you, but I don't know what. I'd like nothing more than to have things like they were before, but you'll have to tell me what's wrong."

His feigned innocence took away any softer feelings she was beginning to have. "Wrong?" She planted her fists on her hips. "Did you really think you could keep it from me?"

His puzzled look would have been convincing if she hadn't learned the sorry truth from Letitia. The act sent her anger over the edge.

"What kind of man buys a wife?"

Michael's head snapped back. "What?"

"You heard me. How low does a man have to sink to send off for a wife like he'd place an order for seeds from a catalog?"

The fire of her anger mounting. "At least a mail-order bride answers an advertisement and enters the bargain of her own accord. Not like your despicable scheme." Her words battered Michael back a step. "How could you possibly believe I wouldn't get wind of this? Did you and the Bartletts believe you could pull the wool over my eyes forever, or was it enough to think you could fool me until after the wedding?"

She could feel her arms shaking and knew that tears weren't far away. She grasped the door handle. "I've been played for a fool, and I don't like it a bit. That's what is wrong!"

The door slammed behind her with a most satisfying crash.

Michael didn't know how long he stared at the closed door. The echo of Elizabeth's words swirled through his brain like a swarm of angry hornets. He tried to make some sense of the flurry of accusations she had flung at him. What was all that about mail-order brides and buying a wife? Had she been talking about herself when she referred to being sent for like some kind of merchandise?

A smile tugged at his lips in spite of his confusion. Merchandise implied something passive, unable to speak for itself. Elizabeth Simmons would never fit that description.

His mood sobered again. From what he could gather, Elizabeth felt she had been the victim of some kind of scheme and, for some reason, had decided he was part of it. And she obviously had no intention of giving him a chance to defend himself.

And where did the Bartletts fit into this? How could she have gotten the notion that he was in league with them? The very idea of being put in the same category as those two made him feel degraded. The last thing he would ever want to do would be to link his lot with the likes of Richard and Letitia Bartlett.

But he knew someone who would.

eighteen

"What do you mean, you hired them to find me a wife?" Michael's bellow reverberated off the walls, but the stocky man facing him seemed unmoved.

"I care about my son and his future. There's no crime in that." Timothy O'Roarke rocked back on his heels and puffed on his half-finished cigar, sending a cloud of gray smoke floating toward the ceiling.

Michael stared at the man he called his father, wondering if it was possible for a person to stray so far that they put themselves beyond God's mercy.

"You don't deny it, then? You admit you offered the Bartletts money to lure some unsuspecting woman out here so I could marry her?"

" 'Lure' has such an unpleasant ring to it. I prefer to think of it as bringing out a likely prospect and allowing nature to take its course." Timothy stroked his mustache with the back of his forefinger. "As it did, you must admit." He hooked his thumbs in his waistcoat pockets and stared at Michael with a benevolent smile.

Michael pulled his collar open. "Did you ever once stop to think how Miss Simmons—how *I*—might feel about being pawns in your little game?"

Timothy swung his hand through the air, waving Michael's objection away with the haze of smoke that wreathed his head. "That's why you weren't meant to know about it," he said in a tone of sweet reason. "I thought you might overreact like this. But all's well that ends well, my boy. I've seen the young lady, and I approve. You do, too, apparently." He lowered his eyelid in a suggestive wink.

Michael gritted his teeth. "Unfortunately, the young lady doesn't approve of your methods any more than I do. Especially since she thinks I was a party to the whole thing. That's why you're going to explain it to her."

The cigar drooped in the corner of Timothy's mouth. "I'm going to. . . No, no. I'm sure she'd rather hear it from you, my boy."

"Unfortunately, she doesn't want to hear anything I have to say at the moment." Michael gripped his father's arm above the elbow and steered him toward the door. "But with your cooperation, I'm hoping that's about to change."

❧

"Any more orders, Jenny?" Elizabeth set two bowls of venison stew on a serving tray and wiped her brow with her forearm.

"That's the lot, for now at least. It looks like things are slowing down for a bit."

"After that rush at lunchtime, I won't complain."

Jenny laughed. "Why don't you sit down for awhile? You look like you could use a break." She picked up the tray and backed through the swinging door. Elizabeth heard her soft gasp and looked up to see Jenny staring into the dining room like one transfixed.

"What's wrong? Another rush?"

Jenny cast a wide-eyed glance over her shoulder. "You could say that." She stepped into the dining room, letting the door swing shut behind her.

A large hand pushed it open on the next swing, and Michael stepped into the room, pushing another man in front of him.

Elizabeth bristled. How dare he enter her restaurant! And straight into her private domain, no less. She opened her mouth to tell him what she thought of his behavior when something about his companion caught her attention.

She took a second look at the man, then a third. What was it about him that triggered that sense of recognition?

A series of scenes came flooding into her mind. Keen eyes

studying her from the corner of the Bartletts' parlor. Eyes that probed and judged her.

His eyes. Her skin crawled, just as it had the first time she'd seen him. Who was this man, and why was he standing in her kitchen? She glared at Michael, her lips pressed together and her chin jutting forward, wordlessly demanding an explanation.

Michael's face wore a grim expression. "There's something you need to know, Elizabeth. Something you need to hear. From him." He indicated his companion with a jerk of his head. "Allow me to introduce you to my father, Timothy O'Roarke."

Timothy? Snippets of remembered comments Richard had made flashed through her mind. So this was the man he'd had to report to when he thought she was unavailable. The same Timothy who refused to pay them off once he found out they had no goods to offer him. The reason for Letitia's abusive diatribe.

And Michael's father? The floor tilted beneath her, and she grasped the edge of the counter to keep from falling.

Michael, his brow wrinkled in concern, hurried to support her, but she dashed his arm aside and forced herself to stand upright. "I don't need your assistance."

Timothy O'Roarke. It made sense, now that all the pieces had been put in place. He had struck the deal with the Bartletts. Only natural that he would come by to check out the merchandise.

Elizabeth could see the physical resemblance, the eyes and hair so like Michael's and yet so different. Her breath quickened, and she felt her strength return as her body responded to her anger. How had they managed to contrive her first meetings with Michael? Timothy must be a master puppeteer. . .and she had been his puppet.

"You need to leave. Both of you." Her voice barely quavered. Good.

"Not until you hear what he has to say." Michael's voice held a ring of authority. He prodded his father's shoulder. "Go on, tell her."

Timothy tugged the gaudy waistcoat down over his ample stomach and cleared his throat. "It's really not as big a thing as the boy makes out," he began. "Just a father trying to do what's best for his son."

He flashed a confident grin at Elizabeth, who glowered at him in return. He shifted his gaze and went on.

"You see, I care about my son here. I've worked hard all my life to carve a niche he could step into. He has what it takes to rise to the top. With a little effort on his part, he could be a part of the legislature, even become a senator once this territory becomes a state.

"Only one thing does he lack, and that's a proper wife. One befitting of the status he will attain. One who knows the ways of polite society and will be an asset to him when he has to move in the right circles back in Washington.

"In a word, someone like you." He paused and looked straight at her now, narrowing his gaze as if waiting for her reaction.

"And so the two of you and the Bartletts cooked up this conspiracy to bring me out here?"

"Well, not exactly." For the first time, Timothy's confidence seemed to waver. "Michael tends to be a bit stubborn about some things. Takes after his mother that way. I had a feeling—just an inkling, you understand—that he might not see the wisdom of what we were about. I thought it would be better if he learned about it later."

"How much later?"

Timothy shrugged as if his coat had suddenly become too small for his thickset frame. "I would have told him when the banns were announced. By the wedding, at the latest."

Elizabeth stared into Michael's blue gaze. "You mean you didn't know? You weren't a party to this?"

His head moved from side to side. "I had no idea. Not until you lit into me about plotting with the Bartletts."

The icy fingers around Elizabeth's heart began to thaw. He hadn't betrayed her trust. He was still the same Michael. Her Michael? The glimmer of hope sent a rush of warmth throughout her being, melting the ice around her heart and washing away the pain.

Timothy's voice broke the silence. "Well, now that it's settled, I'll be on my way." He twirled one end of his mustache and winked at Elizabeth. "All's well that ends well, I always say. And this looks like a fine ending, although I still don't know what Michael was so wrought up about." With a smug look, he strolled out.

Elizabeth watched him go, then turned to Michael. "However can you put up with him?" Her eyes grew wide, and she pressed her hand against her lips, too late to stop the sharp words. Michael didn't seem put off, though, so she took courage and continued. "I'm sorry. I know that's a horrid thing to say about your father, but—"

"You can't possibly say anything about him I haven't said or thought myself." He passed his hand across his face and leaned back against the counter as if welcoming its support.

"My father. . .well, you've seen for yourself. He doesn't play by anyone's rules but his own. And the object of the game is the advancement of Timothy O'Roarke, no matter who or what gets in the way."

"What about this plot he concocted with the Bartletts? Was that for him or for you?"

Michael raked his fingers through his hair. "I'm still trying to figure out how the man's mind works. He has some idea of building a political legacy, and he refuses to believe I'm not willing to become his successor. In his mind, he may honestly believe he's looking out for my best interests. I'm sure he sees me as obstinate and unappreciative, since I don't see things the same way he does."

"Did he follow you out here?"

"No, it was the other way around. When he heard how a new city was being built to serve as the territorial capital, all his political machinations geared up. He pulled every string he could think of to secure an appointment out here. He'd already tasted the beginnings of power back home. He planned to build on that out here for a few years, then head back east trailing streams of glory. He really thinks he's going to build a dynasty. I'm the one who followed him here."

Elizabeth rubbed her arms as though chilled. "But why?" An unsettling thought struck her. "You didn't have political aspirations, too, did you?"

Michael burst out laughing. "Perish the thought! I've seen enough greed and corruption to last me a lifetime. My motives were much simpler—to keep an eye on my father."

"You've taken on quite a burden. It must weigh heavily on you."

"Call it an obligation, if you will. An obligation to my mother's memory." His face lit up at her mention. "She's the one who held our family together. She made sure my sister and I knew we were loved and taught us about a heavenly Father who loved us, too, and would never leave us. All the qualities our earthly father lacked." Michael straightened and stood.

"She's the one who introduced us to Jesus and told us how He could become our Savior. And even after all the years of neglect from our father, she spent hours on her knees, praying for him to come to know the Lord, as well. His behavior sickens me. Sometimes I think I'd like nothing better than to live in a place where no one's ever heard of Timothy O'Roarke and will never know I'm his son." He shoved his hands into his pants pockets.

"But if I did that, I would feel like I'd be turning my back on all my mother's efforts. I can't do that," he stated simply. "If I'm out here, I can reason with him, try to make him see what he's missing. And in the meantime, maybe I can at least keep him from going too far." He shrugged. "Obviously, I haven't done a very good job of that."

Elizabeth moved across the floor to stand directly in front of him. "I think you've done a fine job." She reached up to smooth a dark curl off his forehead.

"You can't make choices for someone else. All you can do is point the way and try to warn them about pitfalls ahead. The rest is up to them." Her voice softened to a whisper. "I think you're a very special man, Michael O'Roarke."

Michael probed her gaze and raised his hand to capture hers where it still lingered near his hairline. Unable to tear her gaze from his, she felt his other hand slide around her shoulders and pull her close.

She rested her cheek against the smooth surface of his shirt. His heartbeat drummed in her ear, keeping time with her own quickening pulse.

The nearest she had come to a man's embrace had been James's brotherly hugs. She didn't want suitors. . .had avoided them, in fact. She was a person in her own right—with no need to diminish her own individuality by merging into the identity of another.

But being wrapped in Michael's arms didn't make her feel diminished. Rather, like two separated parts finally finding each other and becoming a whole.

His fingers cupped her chin and tilted it upward so that she looked into his blue eyes. "And you're a very remarkable woman, Elizabeth Simmons." His gaze seemed to search her heart, questioning, then he lowered his head, and his lips sought hers.

Elizabeth's arms found their way around Michael's broad shoulders, twining around his neck and pulling him closer, finding the other half that made her feel complete. Michael knew her strong will, yet accepted her as she was.

And loved her? The thought sent joy careening through her whole body. She leaned into his embrace. She would sort out her feelings later. For now, it was enough to rest in Michael's arms.

"Is everything all right back here?" Jenny's voice sounded from the doorway. "I thought I smelled something scorching on the stove." Footsteps clattered to a halt. "Oh! Um. . .it looks like the stew has burned. I'll just move it off the stove, shall I?" A pot rattled. "Then I'll. . .I'll just go tidy up the dining room and wait. For customers. Or something." The door swung open, then shut, cutting off the sound of her retreating footsteps.

Michael brushed his lips along her cheek, her ear, her neck. . . . He nestled his head in the hollow of her shoulder. "I suppose we owe her an explanation," he murmured.

Elizabeth nodded. Jenny deserved that.

But it could wait.

nineteen

Michael pushed open the door to the kitchen, where he found Elizabeth wiping down the counters. "Are you about ready to go? I'm eager to hear C. C. Bean's thoughts on the Resurrection. It should be an interesting evening."

"Just let me get a shawl from my room. We can leave as soon as Jenny comes back in from taking the garbage out. We're a little late getting things finished up tonight." She hurried to her room, where she pulled her shawl from its peg, then paused in front of the mirror. She cringed. A day spent over a hot stove had left her hair hanging in limp strands. Michael hadn't mentioned her disheveled appearance, but she wasn't about to go to a Bible study looking like that.

Pulling the pins from her hair, she brushed through it quickly, trying to coax some life back into her chestnut curls. She ran the comb down the center of her head to make a neat part, pulled her hair back on the sides, then secured it in place with two tortoiseshell combs.

She turned her head from side to side to study the effect. Not perfect, but certainly an improvement.

Back in the kitchen, she found Michael scooping a wedge of apple pie from a pan. He looked up with a sheepish grin. "I didn't have much supper. Just thought I'd help with the leftovers."

Elizabeth chuckled and watched him wolf down the slice. It felt good to laugh, good to see Michael at home in her kitchen again, and good to have him back as a part of her life. Life itself was good.

Michael wiped the crumbs from his face and replaced the cloth that covered the pie pan. Elizabeth reached for her reticule. "Ready to go?" she asked.

"I thought we were waiting for Jenny."

"Didn't she come back in yet? I'll go see what's keeping her, while you check the lock on the front door."

She stepped outside into a perfect summer evening. A light breeze from the north caressed her cheek, bringing with it the scent of lilacs. A dove perched in a nearby juniper tree called to another in a piñon pine. It would be a beautiful night for strolling to the Bible study.

"Jenny?" She was probably savoring the lovely evening on her own and had forgotten they were waiting for her.

No answer.

Elizabeth scanned the alleyway, trying to think where Jenny might have gone. She usually stayed well within the shelter of the restaurant's walls, keeping her safe from both snide remarks and the possibility of contact with Martin Lester or Burleigh Ames.

"Jenny?" She called louder this time. Surely Jenny wouldn't have ventured too far afield. Where could she be?

A vague sense of unease settled in the pit of her stomach. She moved past the doorstep to the garbage barrel.

Scraps of food lay scattered across the ground. Her unease blossomed into fear.

"Jenny!" The word floated out into the night but brought no response.

❧

"Michael, she's gone!" Elizabeth stormed into the kitchen, her face flushed and her features taut. The back door banged shut behind her, punctuating her words.

"Gone where?"

"I don't know. She isn't outside. I've looked everywhere. Where can she be?"

"Take it easy. Have you checked her room? Maybe she came in while I was locking the front door and I didn't notice." He followed her to the former storeroom.

Elizabeth tapped on the door, then pushed it open. Michael peered over her shoulder. A cot, neatly made, took up most of the floor space. Jenny's dresses hung from pegs on the walls. A tidy room awaited its occupant's return.

But no sign of Jenny.

Michael caught sight of Elizabeth's trembling lips and laid his hands on her shoulders. "Calm down. There's surely an explanation. Where else could she have gone?"

Elizabeth whirled and clutched his arms. "That's just it. There isn't anyplace else. She—both of us—worried about Ames showing up to bother her. Throwing out the garbage gave her a chance to get outdoors, but it was close enough to be safe. Or so we thought." Her fingers dug into his arms. "Oh, Michael, where is she? What are we going to do?"

He stared down at her hazel eyes, puddled with unshed tears. He'd never seen Elizabeth at a loss before, but now this independent woman was asking for his help, and he knew he had to rise to the occasion.

"Bring that lamp, and let's look outside again. I want to check for tracks, signs. . .anything that might give us a clue." Elizabeth flashed him a grateful smile, picked up the lamp, and followed him outside.

"See?" She pointed at the pile of debris on the ground. "Jenny would never have gone off and left this mess."

Michael nodded, remembering the time she had dropped the garbage. She had made sure every scrap had been picked up before she left. He stood still, letting his gaze roam around the pool of lamplight, trying to get a sense of what must have happened.

"Over here." He strode farther out into the alleyway, where two parallel lines marked the dust. He squatted to examine them more closely.

"Wagon tracks," he stated. "And fresh ones. See how sharp the edges are? Someone came along here not too long ago." He motioned for Elizabeth to wait there and carried the lamp down the alley, following the wagon's progress, careful not to mar any possible signs with his own tracks.

Returning, he noted the print Elizabeth's shoes made and compared them to the other tracks nearby. Those, then, must be Jenny's. And up ahead. . . He drew back, startled.

"What's the matter?" Elizabeth asked.

"It doesn't make sense. I expected to see signs of a struggle. But look at this." He led her a few steps ahead.

"The wagon stopped here." He pointed as he spoke, inviting her to read the story written in the dust. "A man stepped down, but he didn't approach the spot where Jenny stood. Those are her prints, passing behind you and ending up by the wagon."

Elizabeth studied the ground. "That still doesn't tell me where she is."

"Look at this. See that slight shuffling there? That's where they stood and talked. And since her tracks don't lead away. . ." His voice trailed off, and he glanced up at Elizabeth, wondering how to break it to her.

"From everything I see here, it looks like she got into the wagon and rode away of her own free will."

"But that doesn't make sense!" Elizabeth scanned the area, trying to find something that would refute Michael's conclusion. "She wouldn't have gone off like that of her own accord without a word to either one of us."

"I wouldn't have thought so, either. But the evidence shows—"

"I don't care what it shows! Jenny's been living with me, remember? I know her, Michael! She hated having to stay cooped up indoors, but she was terrified her guardian might try to catch her unawares and take her back. The only time she ever came outside was to throw out the garbage or use the privy."

She cast a hopeful glance at the small wooden structure beyond. "Do you think. . . ?"

Michael gave her a look of sympathy but shook his head. "There aren't any fresh prints heading in that direction. The only places she went are the garbage barrel and here."

෨

Elizabeth stared at the footprints in the dust, the final connection Jenny had with this place. She took the lamp from Michael and followed the marks the wagon had left until she reached the end of the alley. No more tracks. No more Jenny.

It was totally unlike Jenny to jump into a wagon and just take off.

As far as you know.

The only people in Prescott Jenny trusted were Elizabeth and Michael.

As far as you know.

"No, I won't believe it." Elizabeth silenced the insidious little voice of doubt. "Something is wrong, Michael. I know what the signs show, but I know Jenny, too." *I do,* she assured herself. "It would be completely out of character for her to up and leave like that. She knew we were waiting for her and that we were just inside the building."

A shiver of apprehension threaded up her spine. It was easy to hear through the restaurant walls. Jenny had only to call out, and they would have rushed to help her. What had happened to keep her from doing just that?

"Get the sheriff, Michael."

He shook his head sorrowfully, and her voice sharpened. "Something is wrong. Go get him."

Michael heaved a sigh. "He's gone. I heard this afternoon. He's off dealing with a dispute over some claim jumpers down around Big Bug."

No. What was he doing, trying to sort out some foolish mining problem when Jenny needed help? Chest heaving, Elizabeth fought for control. "When will he be back?"

"Maybe by morning. Maybe not for days. It all depends on how things go out there."

"We can't wait for days!"

"I know that." He stroked her cheek with the backs of his fingers. "But we're going to have to wait until morning. There's no way we can follow them tonight. I'll check around town, find out if anyone has seen her."

Elizabeth's body stiffened in denial all the while her mind accepted the hard truth of Michael's reasoning.

"We can't trail them until daylight," Michael continued. "But I promise you, I'll be here as soon as the sun comes up."

"Before," Elizabeth demanded. "We need to be ready to leave the moment it's light." She raised her hands, then let them fall to her sides. "I can't just sit around this evening doing nothing, as if she'd gone off to spend the night with a friend."

"Pray that she has." Michael cupped the back of her head in his hand and pulled her close, cradling her against his body as if she were a child. "For that matter, just pray."

❧

By the time Michael tapped on the door the next morning, Elizabeth was dressed and waiting.

"Come inside. The coffee's on." She ushered him in and cast a glance at the overcast sky. Pale gray fingers of light pushed their way through the cloud bank. It wouldn't be long now.

She poured two cups of coffee and sat across the table from Michael, drawing comfort from the warmth of the steaming brew. Even in the summer months, nights grew cold here in the mountains. She shuddered, wondering how Jenny had passed the night.

And where.

Michael cradled his cup in his hands. "Did you come up with any ideas during the night?"

She shook her head slowly. "I have no idea who she would have gone with willingly. Or why."

Only the glimmer of a thought had kept her awake all through the long night hours.

Could Jenny's disappearance have anything to do with seeing the kiss she had shared with Michael the day before?

That Jenny had seen them, she knew without a doubt. Her gasp of surprise and quick departure confirmed that. She hadn't said a word about it later, though, and Elizabeth hadn't found time to explain it to her. Had something about their embrace upset her to the point she would run away without a word?

And if so, what could it be? Elizabeth couldn't think of any reason, save one: What if Jenny cared for Michael herself?

It would be natural enough. After the treatment she had received, first at the hands of Martin Lester, then Burleigh Ames and his customers, any kindness shown by a man would make him seem like her knight in shining armor. Could that account for Jenny's abrupt departure?

"I wonder. . ."

Michael looked up eagerly. "Yes?"

"Never mind." Elizabeth gathered their cups and set them in the basin. She couldn't tell him. Not yet. It was enough to shoulder the burden of guilt at the possibility that her actions might have driven Jenny away. She couldn't bear the shame of admitting it to Michael.

Especially if her suspicions turned out to be true.

"Let's go." She blew out the lamp and stepped outside into the first light of dawn.

On any other morning, she would have gloried in the promise of a new day. Now she felt weighed down by the responsibility of finding Jenny—and the realization that she had no idea what to do first.

"I didn't find anybody who had seen her last night. Let's take a better look at those tracks now that it's daylight." Michael strode to the end of the alley, radiating confidence. She followed, grateful to have a starting point.

"Do they tell you anything?"

"Not much," he admitted. "Only that the wagon turned

west from here. The tracks are so mixed in with the other traffic, I won't be able to follow them."

Elizabeth stared westward, willing herself to spot some sign, some scrap of information that would give them a clue. Except for a few other early risers, the street was empty.

"We'll go that way, then." She walked briskly, putting action to her words. "Someone must have seen them. We just have to find out who."

They queried everyone they met without success until they came upon an old man sweeping his front porch.

"Yesterday evening?" He fingered the tuft of white hair over his right ear. "Sure, I saw a wagon down this way just before sunset. Surprised me some. I thought Lester lived out toward Chino Valley. Don't know what he'd be doing, heading off down the south road."

"Lester?" Misgiving spread through Elizabeth and wrapped itself around her heart. "Martin Lester?"

"That's him. Never did think much of him, to tell you the truth, but that gal with him seemed a nice enough sort."

"A girl?" Dread gripped her heart. Hard. She felt Michael's supporting hand on her back.

"Mm-hm. Pretty little thing, too. Not the type I would have expected to take up with him, if you know what I mean."

Michael saved her from having to respond. "Thanks for the information," he said. He laced his fingers through Elizabeth's and gave them a reassuring squeeze. "At least we know which direction they went."

twenty

"It's wrong, Michael. It doesn't make a bit of sense." Elizabeth shifted on the seat of the wagon Michael had provided and studied the empty landscape in front of them. The early morning clouds had built into thunderheads that covered the afternoon sky.

"If Jenny went off with someone willingly, the last person she'd pick would be Martin Lester. She was terrified of the man." At least she could put to rest her fears that the sight of their embrace had sent Jenny on the run. She clung to that knowledge as her only shred of comfort.

"Whether it makes sense or not, it's the only lead we have." Michael urged the horses forward over the rough terrain. "They were seen together. There's a reason for it; we just don't know what it is yet." He slapped the reins against the horses' rumps and pressed his lips together in a tight line. "But we will."

They pressed on, following the faint trail that had turned off the south road some miles back. Up ahead they spotted a prospector plodding toward them. He stopped and rested his arm on his mule's neck, waiting for them to approach.

"Afternoon," Michael said, pulling the team to a halt.

"Howdy." The grizzled man gazed at them with undisguised interest. "If more folks start coming out this way, I may have to move on to someplace less crowded. Appears this spot is becoming right popular."

"Oh?" Elizabeth could feel Michael's quiver of excitement as he leaned forward. "How's that?"

"You're the second wagon I've seen come through here since morning. Two in one day! This is turning into a regular highway."

Michael's fingers tightened on the reins. "Another wagon, you say? Where was it headed?"

"Same place you are, I reckon." The man tilted his head and regarded them quizzically. "The only thing farther out this way is that old claim Zeb Andrews abandoned six months back. Funny, those other two fellows asked the same question." He slapped his hat against his thigh, sending a cloud of dust into the air. "You'd think if a passel of folks were headed to the same place, they'd have some idea of where they were all going, wouldn't you?"

Elizabeth focused on the only part of his commentary that mattered. "Two fellows? You mean there were two men in the wagon?"

"Yes, Ma'am. Two men and a pile of gear in the back. That and a gunnysack that was squirming to beat the band."

He grinned. "I told them if they were planning to drown a cat, they were looking in the wrong place. There isn't a drop of water in that creek bed that runs through Zeb's old place except when there's a downpour. That's why he up and left." He pushed his tattered hat back on his head and scanned the leaden sky. "This just might be the day it'll catch some rain."

Michael shot a quick glance at Elizabeth. "What did they say about the cat?"

The prospector chuckled. "The driver wasn't real sociable, didn't say much of anything. The fellow with him just laughed and said they had a cat in there, all right. A wildcat that needed taming." He cackled. "Whatever it was, he turned around and cuffed it once, and it settled right back down again."

He wiped his brow, leaving a grimy trail across his forehead. "I don't know, maybe they had a dog they were going to train. Seems funny they'd have it all tied up in a sack like that, but you never can tell about some folks."

"They sound strange, all right," Michael agreed. "The one who did all the talking, what did he look like?"

"Big fellow, broader than you. Looked like a brawler. Kind of a sour type, except for the one time he laughed. Friend of yours?"

"No," Michael said. "I wouldn't say that."

The man peered into the back of their wagon, empty save for canteens of water and some food Elizabeth had hastily packed. "You ain't planning to train no dogs, I see. You out hunting or something?"

"We might be." Michael's tone was ominous. "We just might be." He shook the reins, and the horses started off, then Michael turned around and called back over his shoulder, "How far ahead is that claim you mentioned?"

"Couple of miles or so. Not much there, just a dried-up creek and Zeb's old shack."

"Much obliged." Michael settled back in the seat and clucked at the horses.

"Are we on the right track?" Elizabeth asked. "He said two men."

Michael nodded with a grim expression. "Did you recognize the description of the second man?"

Elizabeth shook her head.

"I did. It fits Burleigh Ames like a glove."

"From the Nugget?" She looked at Michael with a growing sense of horror. "Then the bag in the back of their wagon. . ."

"Was Jenny."

A wave of numbness shrouded Elizabeth's brain. Maybe it would have been better if Jenny had run away. She could feel anger then, hurt and disappointment, instead of this feeling of being caught in a nightmare that wouldn't end.

"How much farther?"

"Less than a mile now. Just before we reach the top of that rise, we'll leave the wagon and walk the rest of the way."

A thought struck her. "You did leave word for the sheriff, didn't you?"

Michael hesitated a moment. "No."

Elizabeth jerked back as if she'd been slapped. "What? If he gets back from Big Bug anytime soon, he can head out here to help us."

Michael guided the horses away from the track and headed them into a clump of manzanita. "Not much cover," he said, "but it's the best we're going to get."

He took his time setting the brake, then faced her squarely. "There's something you need to understand. Martin Lester is Jenny's legal guardian, duly appointed by her father. And she's only eighteen, still a minor. In the eyes of the law, he has every right to take her back."

Elizabeth gaped. "After the things he's done? Surely—"

Michael laid his fingers across her lips. "But he never actually did anything prosecutable. The law won't hang a man for what he threatens to do, only for what he succeeds in doing. Even if the sheriff were here right now, his hands would be tied."

Thunder rumbled in the distance. "Then that means. . ."

Michael nodded. "We're on our own."

❧

"That's the place?" Elizabeth stared at the sorry excuse for a cabin in the hollow below them.

"It has to be," Michael answered. "I can see the tail of their wagon sticking out past the corner."

Elizabeth rubbed her ankles, tender after their hike, and took stock of their position.

On the far side of the ramshackle structure, a dry creek bed meandered off into the distance. Between the rolling hilltops and the basin where the cabin lay, the slopes held only grass, the sole exception being the cluster of small juniper trees where she and Michael had concealed themselves.

"How are we going to cross that open ground without them seeing us?"

"We can't," he said. "We'll have to wait for nightfall."

"That's hours away yet! Think about what could be

happening to Jenny in the meantime. They may not even be expecting anyone to be tailing them."

"I'm not about to take that chance." Michael held up his hand to still Elizabeth's protest. "Let's say I leave you here and make it to the cabin without being seen. That still leaves them with a two-to-one advantage. And they have Jenny."

He leaned back against a juniper trunk and stretched his legs out in front of him. "And that's assuming I make it. Let's say they spot me before I reach the shack. Not only can they pick me off at their leisure, but that leaves both you and Jenny alone out here, at their mercy, and with no hope of rescue. I'm not going to risk either one of you like that."

"So if you wait until dark and get down there safely, then what?"

Michael smiled. "Then the odds will be different. I'll have you with me."

"You didn't really expect I'd stay behind, did you?"

"Chivalry says I ought to leave you here or even take you back to town and return here myself, maybe with more men. But there's no guarantee Ames and Lester wouldn't be gone by the time I got back. And to tell the truth, Elizabeth, there's no one I'd rather have backing me up than you."

That declaration sustained her all through the long hours of waiting, with the two of them sheltered beneath the junipers. Elizabeth impatiently traced the course of the sun across the sky, passing the time by making plans with Michael.

And praying. Prayers for Jenny, that somehow she would be protected during their enforced wait. For her and Michael, that the rescue they had worked out would go without a hitch, bringing Jenny back to safety and keeping the three of them safe.

Prayers for the two men inside the cabin came harder. *I know You love them, Lord, no matter what they've done. You died for them, just like You did for me. But I just can't find it in myself to feel much compassion for them right now.*

The sun set with agonizing slowness. Elizabeth watched its descent toward the horizon, willing it to hurry up and drop behind the mountaintops.

Shadows lengthened and stretched across the barren ground from the distant hills, finally reaching the hollow where their objective lay.

The time had come. Finally! Elizabeth sat up under the sheltering branches and stretched. She welcomed the chance to do something tangible. She dreaded it just as much.

Beside her, Michael checked the loads in his pistol and shoved two brass shells into the shotgun at his side. "Ready?"

Even with the cover of darkness, their movement across the open ground felt all too exposed. Elizabeth watched the cabin window, now glowing with lamplight, for signs of anyone keeping watch. An occasional shadow crossed the opening, but no one stopped or looked out.

At the edge of the grass, Michael reached for her arm and pulled her to a stop. "This is where we separate," he whispered, drawing her close. "Do you remember everything?"

She nodded. They had gone over their plan often enough during the weary hours of waiting.

He placed the shotgun in her hands. "Remember, it's going to take me awhile to lead their horses a distance away. While I'm gone, I want you just to sit tight. Don't try anything on your own." He gathered her in his arms and held her tight. "Promise me you'll be careful. It ought to work, but there's always the possibility of something going wrong. Whatever happens, take care of yourself. If anything happened to you. . ." He seized her shoulders and pressed his lips to hers in a brief, hard kiss. Then he was gone.

Elizabeth waited a moment, listening to the faint rustle as his boots swept through the grass. The hint of a breeze grazed her cheek. Over near the creek bed, a lone cricket set up a steady chirping.

And in the cabin, Jenny waited. The thought spurred

Elizabeth into action. Making no more noise than Michael had, she slipped through the shadows until she reached the end of the shack. The cricket ceased its chirping; otherwise, nothing else seemed to take note of her nocturnal prowling.

She flattened herself against the weathered wall and edged toward the open window. Her foot caught on an object, and she reached down to probe the obstruction with her fingers. A half-buried tin can stuck up out of the ground. She stepped around it, careful to make no sound. Evidently, Zeb hadn't been too careful about keeping the place picked up. She crept ahead on her hands and knees, the shotgun making her progress awkward.

Voices murmured through the window. Elizabeth reached her goal and sat beneath it, trying to control the trembling in her limbs. Michael should have reached the horses by now.

The windowsill lay just inches above her head. Did she dare rise up and look inside? She balanced on the balls of her feet and inched upward, then jerked to a stop. Elizabeth yanked impatiently at the hem of her skirt, where it had gotten caught under the toes of her shoes.

She tried again, feeling the sharpness of the rough-cut wood as her fingers crept up the wall. Her head had just reached the level of the windowsill when a man's back appeared in the opening. She ducked back down out of sight, panting, and strained to hear what was going on inside.

Boots scraped across the floor. She heard the clatter of dishes, and the scent of bacon drifted out into the night.

"About time we got fed."

Elizabeth froze, focusing her attention on the deep voice.

"Right about that," the second man responded in a higher-pitched tone. "I was about to starve. It's hard to think straight when your belly's empty. She can cook, anyway. At least she's good for something."

Elizabeth let out a sigh. At least Jenny was still alive, from the sounds of it.

"She better be good for more than that. I traded you that whiskey in good faith, and I need to get something back on my investment. And I don't mean singing."

So the deeper voice belonged to Burleigh Ames. That meant Martin Lester possessed the high, whiny tone.

"You will, you will," Lester assured him. "Just give her time to warm up to the notion. I found this place and got her out here for you, didn't I?"

"For all the good it's done us so far. She hasn't even said a word."

"We just needed a place out away from people and a little time to convince her that life will be a whole lot easier if she gets over her highfalutin' ways and decides to cooperate."

Ames grunted. "She'd better get around to cooperating pretty soon. I've got a business to run."

"Don't worry. She gets hungry enough, and she'll come around. Fixing all that food for us when she hasn't had a bite to eat since I picked her up last night should persuade her soon enough." Lester snickered.

Ames responded with a rumbling chuckle that made Elizabeth's blood run cold. How much longer would it take Michael to lead the horses far enough away?

"Just like breaking a horse, I reckon," Ames said. "With some, you've gotta use more persuasion. Hey!" His voice sharpened. "Get away from the door!" Footsteps pounded on the wooden floor.

"You get back there and clean up the supper dishes," Lester snarled. "If you decide to sweeten up and change your tune, we might let you eat breakfast with us in the morning. You're fixing flapjacks, did I tell you? And I brought some eggs along, too. Or you can be stubborn and wait until lunch. Or dinner. Or the middle of next week, for all I care." His voice took on a more threatening note. "Or we can stake you out somewhere and leave you for the Apaches to find. What do you think about that?"

His menacing tone changed to a yelp of alarm. Elizabeth heard a loud, clanging noise, followed by a series of scrambling sounds and angry yells. Only her fear of getting ahead of the plan and spoiling their chances kept her from jumping up to peer through the window.

"I told you to stay away from that door!" Ames's bellow cut through the room. "Tie her in that chair again. We can't take a chance on her getting away."

"I'll teach you to sling a pan of hot grease at me," Lester shouted. "Get over here and sit down. I'll snug these ropes up so tight you won't get another chance to run, you little wildcat."

"Watch her teeth!" Ames called.

Lester cursed. Elizabeth heard the sound of a hand striking flesh, followed by a cry from Jenny.

"Maybe now you'll keep still."

Elizabeth clamped her lower lip between her teeth. If Michael didn't come back soon, she would be sorely tempted to take action on her own.

"Here," Ames said. "Have something to settle your nerves."

Glasses clinked, and Elizabeth could hear liquid gurgling. Liquor on top of their already violent mood?

Hurry, Michael!

twenty-one

Michael slid out of the darkness as if in answer to her silent call and pressed his mouth close to her ear. "Have you been able to look inside?" he asked in a barely audible whisper.

"No." She kept her voice as low as his. "But I've heard more than enough." She quickly recounted what had transpired and could tell Michael's anger equaled her own.

"If they've started drinking, we can't afford to waste any time. Are you ready?"

Elizabeth nodded. After what she had just listened to, she was more than eager to see their plan through.

She gripped the stock of the shotgun in both hands and crouched beneath the window. Michael should just about have had enough time to reach the door. Any moment, he would kick it open.

There! She heard the sound of splintering wood and the crash as the door slammed back against the wall. She sprang to her feet in time to see both men leap back in surprise and reach for their guns.

"I wouldn't," she called.

Their heads swiveled toward the sound of her voice, any temptation to discount a mere woman's order nullified by the twin barrels she aimed at them.

"What do you think you're doing, busting in here like that?" the scrawny one yelled. Elizabeth pegged him for Martin Lester. She recognized the other from the description the prospector had given them: Burleigh Ames. Even from across the room, the man emanated a sense of malice.

But where was Jenny? She hadn't made a sound since her cry of pain, and Elizabeth couldn't see her from where she stood.

"Just keep your hands in the air," Michael ordered. To Elizabeth, he called, "You can come inside now."

She ran to the front of the cabin and joined him in the single room. The men stood next to their overturned chairs behind a rickety table where a lamp flickered. To her left was a rusty cookstove.

And over near the far wall sat Jenny, bound hand and foot to a chair. Even in the dim glow of the lamp, the bright red imprint of a hand showed clearly on her cheek. Her head drooped listlessly. Was she unconscious or merely dazed from the blow she'd received?

Elizabeth edged toward her, keeping her shotgun aimed toward Lester and Ames.

"Both of you, throw down your guns and get over there against the wall," Michael said.

Two pistols thudded to the floor, and the men stepped back slowly. "Ain't no call for you to be interfering," Lester whined. "We're just trying to reclaim what's rightfully ours."

Michael's expression could have been carved out of stone. "Guardianship doesn't give you the right to abuse a woman. We aren't about to stand by and let that happen."

"Ames!" Michael hollered at the big man. "Move away from the window. Elizabeth, keep them covered while I find something to tie them with." He rummaged through the goods Jenny's abductors had piled in a corner.

Burleigh Ames lifted his left hand, which still held the bottle of whiskey. "You won't begrudge me a last drink before you truss me up, will you?" He raised his arm slowly, then drew it back and flung the bottle straight at Michael.

Elizabeth shouted a warning. Michael jumped to one side. The bottle hit the lamp, then both rolled off the table and across the floor in a spray of whiskey, flame, and shattered glass.

In the near darkness, Elizabeth saw Ames dive for his gun. Michael kicked it out of the way. Ames then reached for Michael, and the two grappled and rolled across the floor.

Flames licked up the wall, catching the tattered tarp that hung near the window and spreading into a blaze.

"Michael!" she screamed. "We've got to get out of here!" The place was a tinderbox. It wouldn't take more than a few minutes for the whole shack to be consumed. Fighting desperately to keep his gun hand out of Burleigh's reach, he didn't answer.

Martin Lester started toward the door. "Hold it right there," she told him. "You don't move until I tell you to."

"Elizabeth?"

She glanced over her shoulder. Jenny stared at the floor, unable to move away from the flames that crept dangerously close to the hem of her skirt. Elizabeth saw movement at the edge of her vision and swung back around. Lester had taken advantage of her momentary distraction and was on the floor scrabbling for his gun.

No time for orders or threats. In one fluid movement, she brought the barrel of the shotgun down on his head, producing a dull thud. He dropped flat and lay still.

"Elizabeth!" Jenny, fully alert now, was straining away from the flames with terror-filled eyes.

Elizabeth wrapped her arms around Jenny's body and dragged her backward, chair and all. She dropped to her knees and pulled frantically at the ropes.

"Knife. By the stove." Jenny's voice came in staccato bursts.

By the stove. . . There it was! Elizabeth seized it and raced back to Jenny. She sawed through the ropes with relative ease, giving thanks for the sharp blade.

When the last strand had been cut, she pulled Jenny out of the chair. Jenny sagged against her, and she braced herself to support the girl's weight.

"Get her out!" Michael yelled.

She had no problem finding her way to the door. The flames that now covered two walls and threatened a third bathed the cabin in a bright yellow light.

She half-carried, half-dragged Jenny to a spot a safe distance from the burning shack. She sat Jenny down and set the shotgun beside her, then turned back to the blazing building—Michael was still inside.

She raced back to the doorway, pushing forward despite the heat of the flames. Burleigh Ames had both hands wrapped around Michael's throat, slowly choking the life out of him.

Elizabeth grabbed the chair Jenny had occupied and raised it high above her head. With every ounce of strength she possessed, she brought it down on Burleigh Ames's shoulders.

He reared back with a loud bellow, loosening his hold on Michael, who pulled his fist back and flattened Ames with a crushing blow to the temple. Elizabeth backed out the door as Michael seized the unconscious man's collar and dragged him outside. Martin Lester roused and stumbled out the door behind them seconds before the roof collapsed, sending a shower of sparks skyward.

&

Michael returned with the wagon just as Burleigh Ames sat up and moaned. Elizabeth sat guard with the shotgun, covering both him and Martin Lester.

Michael scooped Jenny up as if she weighed no more than a sack of feathers and laid her in the back of the wagon. He turned to Elizabeth and lifted her to the seat. "Time to go home," he said.

"Wait a minute," Lester called. "What about us?"

Michael stepped up to the wagon seat and gave him a look of contempt. "Consider yourselves lucky to be alive."

"You don't mean you're going to leave us here? Where's our horses?"

"Halfway to Prescott," Michael said. He pulled a canteen from the wagon bed behind him and tossed it onto the ground near Lester's feet.

"You can't take her from me! I know my rights."

"You'd better ration that water," Michael told him. "It's a long walk home. It should give both of you plenty of time to think about those rights of yours." A rumble of thunder rolled across the sky. "And I'd get started soon, if I were you. It looks like it's going to rain any time now."

The moon shone in the eastern sky, still free of the clouds that were blowing in from the west. Elizabeth blessed the fact that it gave them light to retrace their path back to the south road. She looked at Jenny's slender form, huddled in the wagon bed.

"Are you all right?" A stupid thing to ask, considering all the girl had gone through, but she needed to hear something from Jenny's lips.

She stared up at Elizabeth. "How did you get away to come find me? I can't go back to town with you."

"Get away? What do you mean?"

"Martin Lester drove around back when I was taking out the trash last night. It nearly scared me to death when I saw who it was. He told me Burleigh had gone in the front door and had you tied up inside. He said Burleigh would kill you if I didn't go with him."

"Oh, Honey! So that's why you went off with him without a fight." She leaned over to stroke Jenny's hair. "That didn't happen. It was all a lie."

Jenny's countenance crumpled. "I should have known. He never told me the truth about anything before. . .except when he said he was trading me to Burleigh." She reached up for Elizabeth's hand and squeezed it. "I was so scared."

"So were we, Honey. So were we."

Jenny's fingers relaxed their grip. "She's asleep," Elizabeth told Michael.

"She has to be exhausted after what she's been through." He put his arm around Elizabeth and pulled her head to his shoulder. "You probably are, too. Why don't you try to sleep on the way back?"

"I couldn't possibly. I'm still too stirred up."

The next thing she knew, Michael was shaking her gently. "We're home," he said. She let him help her down, then held the door open while he carried Jenny to her room.

After he left the room, she helped Jenny undress and put her to bed. When she came back into the kitchen, Michael had coffee ready.

"How is she?"

Elizabeth rested her elbow on the table and propped her head on her hand. "Physically, I'd say she's all right. A little banged up from being bounced around in the back of Martin Lester's wagon, but nothing a good night's sleep and a few days of rest won't cure. As far as her thinking, though. . ." Her voice trailed off.

"It's only natural for her to be scared. She's been through quite an ordeal."

"She isn't scared, Michael. She's angry."

"At Lester and Ames? That may be a good thing. Anger's more of a tonic than fear any day."

"Not at them. At God. According to her, this is just one more time He let her down."

Michael leaned back in his chair. "Wait a minute. What about Him leading us right to her and keeping her protected all that time? Doesn't He get any credit for that?"

Elizabeth shook her head wearily. "The way she sees it, He could have kept them from nabbing her in the first place, but He didn't. Further proof in her mind that while He may love everybody else, He doesn't love Jenny Davis." She laced her fingers together so tightly her knuckles turned white. "What should I do? I don't know how to reach her."

Michael reached across the table and covered both her hands with his. "You once told me you can't force a person to believe. You can only point the way for them. I think that applies here as well."

"Maybe. But I'm not giving up on her."

A glimmer of laughter sparked in his eyes. "I never for a moment thought that you would."

Without moving the hand covering hers, Michael scooted his chair closer and leaned toward her. "Jenny isn't the only one who was scared tonight."

Her hand tightened under his. "What do you mean?"

"When I was on the floor, wrestling with Burleigh Ames, I looked up and saw you standing in the middle of that inferno. It occurred to me that maybe neither one of us would make it out of there." He stroked the back of her hand with his thumb.

She searched his eyes. "And that scared you?"

"More than you can imagine. You know what else scares me? The idea of living the rest of my life without you." He pushed back his chair and stood, pulling her up with him.

"I know you treasure your independence. Your strength is one of the things I admire most about you. God placed us both here and brought us together. It seems to me He must have had a reason."

He lifted both her hands in his and pressed them against his heart. "I know this isn't the setting we would have had back home. I would have asked for your father's consent and come to you with a ring in my pocket. And I'm sure your mother would be shocked at the idea of me proposing to you in your kitchen. Although," he added with a smile that sent a glow flowing through her like warm honey, "I can't think of a more pleasant place to be."

Raising her hands to his lips, he kissed each fingertip. "I guess there's another thing that scares me, and that's the possibility that you may say no. But what scares me even more is the thought I should have asked you and didn't." Keeping his gaze locked on hers, he bent down on one knee.

"I love you, Elizabeth. Love you and admire you for your courage and your spirit. I can't imagine life without you. Will you marry me?"

When had the tears started flowing down her cheeks? She looked down at her dear Michael's face.. Here was a man who accepted her as she was. The man God had put in her life. The man she wanted in her life forever. "I'd be honored to," she whispered.

Michael bounded to his feet and wrapped his arms around her in a crushing embrace. "Thank You, Lord," she heard him whisper. Then he lowered his head to hers and kissed her with an intensity that drove all other thoughts from her mind.

❧

Dear Carrie,

You've complained that I haven't included enough adventure in my letters of late. Settle back in a comfortable chair, dear sister, for what I am about to relate will satisfy even your romantic soul. . . .

A Letter To Our Readers

Dear Reader:

In order that we might better contribute to your reading enjoyment, we would appreciate your taking a few minutes to respond to the following questions. We welcome your comments and read each form and letter we receive. When completed, please return to the following:

Fiction Editor
Heartsong Presents
PO Box 719
Uhrichsville, Ohio 44683

1. Did you enjoy reading *Land of Promise* by Carol Cox?
❑ Very much! I would like to see more books by this author!
❑ Moderately. I would have enjoyed it more if

_____

_____

_____

2. Are you a member of Heartsong Presents? ❑ Yes ❑ No
If no, where did you purchase this book? _____

_____

3. How would you rate, on a scale from 1 (poor) to 5 (superior), the cover design? _____

4. On a scale from 1 (poor) to 10 (superior), please rate the following elements.

____ Heroine   ____ Plot
____ Hero   ____ Inspirational theme
____ Setting   ____ Secondary characters

5. These characters were special because?_____

_____

_____

6. How has this book inspired your life?_____

_____

_____

7. What settings would you like to see covered in future
   Heartsong Presents books? _____

_____

_____

8. What are some inspirational themes you would like to see
   treated in future books? _____

_____

_____

9. Would you be interested in reading other Heartsong
   Presents titles? ❑ Yes   ❑ No

10. Please check your age range:
    ❑ Under 18   ❑ 18-24
    ❑ 25-34   ❑ 35-45
    ❑ 46-55   ❑ Over 55

Name _____

Occupation _____

Address _____

City_____ State_____ Zip_____

HIGHLAND
Legacy

4 stories in 1

*F*our generations of love are rooted in Scotland. When Audrey MacMurray seeks her Scottish roots, she uncovers the lives of brave, romantic women during the 1300s, 1700s, and 1800s. Authors include: Tracey V. Bateman, Pamela Griffin, Tamela Hancock Murray, and Jill Stengl.

Historical, paperback, 352 pages, 5 ³/₁₆"x 8"

❤ ❤ ❤ ❤ ❤ ❤ ❤ ❤ ❤ ❤ **❤** ❤ ❤ ❤ ❤ ❤ ❤ ❤ ❤ ❤

❤ ❤ ❤ ❤ ❤ ❤ ❤ ❤ ❤ ❤ **❤** ❤ ❤ ❤ ❤ ❤ ❤ ❤ ❤ ❤

Hearts❤ng

Presents

___HP460 *Sweet Spring*, M. H. Flinkman
___HP463 *Crane's Bride*, L. Ford
___HP464 *The Train Stops Here*, G. Sattler
___HP467 *Hidden Treasures*, J. Odell
___HP468 *Tarah's Lessons*, T. V. Bateman
___HP471 *One Man's Honor*, L. A. Coleman
___HP472 *The Sheriff and the Outlaw*,
       K. Comeaux
___HP475 *Bittersweet Bride*, D. Hunter
___HP476 *Hold on My Heart*, J. A. Grote
___HP479 *Cross My Heart*, C. Cox
___HP480 *Sonoran Star*, N. J. Farrier
___HP483 *Forever Is Not Long Enough*,
       B. Youree
___HP484 *The Heart Knows*, E. Bonner
___HP488 *Sonoran Sweetheart*, N. J. Farrier
___HP491 *An Unexpected Surprise*, R. Dow
___HP492 *The Other Brother*, L. N. Dooley
___HP495 *With Healing in His Wings*,
       S. Krueger
___HP496 *Meet Me with a Promise*, J. A. Grote
___HP499 *Her Name Was Rebekah*,
       B. K. Graham
___HP500 *Great Southland Gold*, M. Hawkins
___HP503 *Sonoran Secret*, N. J. Farrier
___HP504 *Mail-Order Husband*, D. Mills
___HP507 *Trunk of Surprises*, D. Hunt
___HP508 *Dark Side of the Sun*, R. Druten
___HP511 *To Walk in Sunshine*, S. Laity

___HP512 *Precious Burdens*, C. M. Hake
___HP515 *Love Almost Lost*, I. B. Brand
___HP516 *Lucy's Quilt*, J. Livingston
___HP519 *Red River Bride*, C. Coble
___HP520 *The Flame Within*, P. Griffin
___HP523 *Raining Fire*, L. A. Coleman
___HP524 *Laney's Kiss*, T. V. Bateman
___HP531 *Lizzie*, L. Ford
___HP532 *A Promise Made*, J. L. Barton
___HP535 *Viking Honor*, D. Mindrup
___HP536 *Emily's Place*, T. Victoria Bateman
___HP539 *Two Hearts Wait*, F. Chrisman
___HP540 *Double Exposure*, S. Laity
___HP543 *Cora*, M. Colvin
___HP544 *A Light Among Shadows*, T. H. Murray
___HP547 *Maryelle*, L. Ford
___HP548 *His Brother's Bride*, D. Hunter
___HP551 *Healing Heart*, R. Druten
___HP552 *The Vicar's Daughter*, K. Comeaux
___HP555 *But For Grace*, T. V. Bateman
___HP556 *Red Hills Stranger*, M. G. Chapman
___HP559 *Banjo's New Song*, R. Dow
___HP560 *Heart Appearances*, P. Griffin
___HP563 *Redeemed Hearts*, C. M. Hake
___HP564 *Tender Hearts*, K. Dykes
___HP567 *Summer Dream*, M. H. Flinkman
___HP568 *Loveswept*, T. H. Murray
___HP571 *Bayou Fever*, K. Y'Barbo
___HP572 *Temporary Husband*, D. Mills

Great Inspirational Romance at a Great Price!

Heartsong Presents books are inspirational romances in contemporary and historical settings, designed to give you an enjoyable, spirit-lifting reading experience. You can choose wonderfully written titles from some of today's best authors like Peggy Darty, Sally Laity, Tracie Peterson, Colleen L. Reece, Debra White Smith, and many others.

When ordering quantities less than twelve, above titles are $3.25 each.
Not all titles may be available at time of order.

$\mathcal{H}$EARTSONG 💜 PRESENTS

Love Stories Are Rated G!

That's for godly, gratifying, and of course, great! If you love a thrilling love story but don't appreciate the sordidness of some popular paperback romances, **Heartsong Presents** is for you. In fact, **Heartsong Presents** is the premiere inspirational romance book club featuring love stories where Christian faith is the primary ingredient in a marriage relationship.

Sign up today to receive your first set of four, never-before-published Christian romances. Send no money now; you will receive a bill with the first shipment. You may cancel at any time without obligation, and if you aren't completely satisfied with any selection, you may return the books for an immediate refund!

Imagine. . .four new romances every four weeks—two historical, two contemporary—with men and women like you who long to meet the one God has chosen as the love of their lives. . .all for the low price of $10.99 postpaid.

To join, simply complete the coupon below and mail to the address provided. **Heartsong Presents** romances are rated G for another reason: They'll arrive Godspeed!

YES! Sign me up for Hearts💜ng!

NEW MEMBERSHIPS WILL BE SHIPPED IMMEDIATELY!
Send no money now. We'll bill you only $10.99 post-paid with your first shipment of four books. Or for faster action, call toll free 1-800-847-8270.

NAME_____

ADDRESS_____

CITY_____STATE_____ ZIP_____

MAIL TO: HEARTSONG PRESENTS, P.O. Box 721, Uhrichsville, Ohio 44683
or visit www.heartsongpresents.com